DEGREES
FOR
EVERYONE

Also by Bob Jones

Novels:
The Permit (1984)
Full Circle (2000)
Ogg (2002)
True Facts (2003)

Non-fiction:
NZ's Boxing Yearbook 1972
NZ's Boxing Yearbook 1973

Jones on Property (1977)
NZ The Way I Want It (1978)
Travelling (1980)
Bob Jones Letters (1982)
Bob Jones Eighties Letters (1990)
Prosperity Denied (1996)
Memories of Muldoon (1997)

Essays:
Wimp Walloping (1989)
Prancing Pavonine Charlatans (1990)
A Year of It (1991)
Punch Lines (1992)
Wowser Whacking (1993)

DEGREES
FOR
EVERYONE

BOB JONES

HAZARD PRESS
publishers

As always, any resemblance to any living person in name or description is a truely astonishing coincidence.

ISBN 1-877270-70-9

Cover design: Working Ideas
Cover illustration and calligraphy: Lorraine Brady

Published by Hazard Press Limited
P.O. Box 2151, Christchurch, New Zealand
email: info@hazard.co.nz
www.hazardonline.com
Printed by Astra Print, Wellington

PROLOGUE

WHEN IN 1786 the Tenth Duke Of Ralston fell and split his skull while fox hunting in his cups, concern arose about his successor. For the Eleventh Duke, then aged 24, was already a source of gossip for his puzzlingly effete tastes. Not for him lay pleasure in the expected ducal role of a "sportsman" – of drunken wenching visits to London, then a full day's travel and forty miles from Ralston village; nor the patronage of pugilists, or hunting, feasting, rent-collecting and overseeing the management of the 6,500-acre ducal estate. Instead, on learning of his father's death he reluctantly farewelled his Oxford tutors and returned to assume his duties at Ralston.

But years of absorption in mediaeval philosophy was an addiction not easily discarded. It was therefore little surprise when two years later, following consultation with his former tutors, the young Duke set aside fifty acres in the picturesque Ralston valley and, in fine Cornish stone, constructed Ralston University to advance further mediaeval philosophical scholarship and thus allow him to continue with his passion.

In its first three decades the university was confined to mediaeval philosophy and the classics, and as its reputation grew it attracted serious-minded students from across the land. In line with this growth the village also expanded through demand for maids, porters, cooks, laundry staff, gardeners and other menial roles at the university.

In 1832 the Eleventh Duke died in his bed, clutching a copy of his revered Augustine's *City of God*. Anticipating his eventual demise, and conscious of his offsprings' reversion to type in their rejection of intellectual pursuits, he had long since established an endowment fund and an administrative body to ensure the university's continuation.

Over the next six decades, in accord with the new Victorian spirit of expansion, the university widened its horizons, introducing science, mathematics, English literature, general philosophy and history departments.

By the advent of the twentieth century, and despite its new courses, Ralston's reputation as a classical scholarship establishment commanded respect – although not admiration, for its students were mainly aspiring clergymen.

During the latter years of the Great War the university gained a fleeting notoriety as a source of poetic idealism, but the onset of 1920s hedonism soon relegated it to its former obscurity.

When the Fourteenth Duke expired in 1958 his successor dealt with the ruinous introduction of death duties by passing the university to the state in settlement of his tax bill. By then Ralston village had grown to a town numbering 15,000, following expansion of the stockbroker belt into its terrain and completion of a motorway placing it a mere 30 minutes from London.

Throughout the 1980s low-income housing spread across the valley and Ralston village's formerly rustic vista, dominated by the university's ivy-clad clock tower and church spire, was now overwhelmed by a five-level chocolate factory constructed in the then voguish brutalist style.

Ralston's population quickly rose to 45,000 and, proud of its boast as Britain's chocolate capital, the town council actively promoted its industrial attractions with only a passing reference to the university in its publicity material. For in its two centuries of existence no prime minister, Nobel Prize winner, acclaimed artist, author or admiral had emerged from Ralston University's portals. Instead it had provided a steady flow of nondescript schoolmasters, clerics and civil servants, and its only public-figure alumni were three bishops, one Olympian (42nd in the 1928 marathon), a poisoning parson hanged in 1926 for the murder of six elderly parishioners, and a bevy of backbench parliamentarians, magistrates and minor town councillors. Only in one respect was the university internationally renowned, although to the general public and even the broader academic world it was a regard so esoteric as to be unworthy of attention. That narrow fame was in the veneration held by mediaeval philosophy scholars across the globe for the Ralston mediaeval philosophy library, housed in Anselm Hall and generally considered to be the second most important in the world. Within the library was a visiting scholars' reading room. Required volumes would be requested and signed for then recovered at day's end with a further signing rigmarole, all under the eye of a librarian dedicated solely to this supervisory function. A maximum of eight such pilgrims were permitted at any one time, resulting in an ever-lengthening waiting time for access.

Despite its academic insignificance outside of mediaeval philosophy, the university rapidly expanded in the 1990s by introducing the fashionable new pseudo-science subjects of psychology and sociology and, in due course, the non-subjects of commerce and business administration.

Consistent with its peers across the land, by the end of the twentieth century Ralston was mired in debt following fourteen successive years of ever-increasing deficits.

After briefly flirting with turning the university into an asylum for which the exploding output of psychologists, psychiatrists and grief counsellors were creating a parallel demand, Whitehall decided to give Ralston one last chance. The University Council was replaced by prominent City sharebrokers and merchant bankers, with the single brief to place Ralston on a firm financial footing with a view to eventual privatization.

The new Council promptly sacked the Vice-Chancellor and engaged consultants to find his replacement, with the emphatic instruction to appoint a man of "hard-headed, no-nonsense, financial experience". And so the story begins.

CHAPTER ONE

PROFESSOR TROUT ROSE from his armchair and, fixing his gaze high on his study's book-lined rear wall, spread his arms with the cultivated thespianism of the life-long pedagogue.

"You may consider," he intoned with an affected and distant air, "that this first application of Porphyrian logic early in the tenth century marked a watershed in theological disputation. It certainly led, by the then-prevailing standards, to a new thinking in mediaeval philosophy, namely …?" Pausing, he raised his eyebrows quizzically at the avid faces of his four post-graduate mediaeval philosophy students. The Chicago Rhodes scholar, Theopopolus, predictably spoke up first. The Professor braced himself for the usual tiresome debate with the American, whose contrariness over the most trivial observations had been a distasteful irritant in the seminars throughout the year.

"You're referring to the nominalists, Prof. But surely if one's to apply the term 'watershed' then one must really favour Anselm. After all, he …" But Theopopolus's argumentative discourse was abruptly interrupted by a ghetto-blaster blaring at full volume beneath the study's open window. A moronic negro voice chanted in a snarling staccato monotone:

Find the truth mon in the 'hood,
Fuckin' pigs doan understood,
Black brothers link in common soul
White filth keep them in their hole,
Brothers …

Belying his six decades Professor Trout darted athleticly to the window and slammed it shut.

Outside on the two-centuries-old lawn, beneath the autumn-hued ancient oaks, small groups of Arab, African and Indian male students loitered, the Africans all wearing dark glasses, the Arabs fingering cellphones and the Indians their noses. The ghetto-blaster owner, an absurdly dressed dreadlocked black youth wearing what the Professor took to be a tea cosy on his head, could be seen jerking marionette-like about his radio, now on the ground.

Professor Trout looked at his watch. Dammit, five o'clock already, and with a dismissive gesture he signalled an end to the session. "We'll resume at two tomorrow," he said sharply, and sensing his mood change the four students rose and quietly departed. Clearly there would be no post-seminar sherry served today.

The Professor turned again to the window and watched

gloomily as from the portals of Anselm Hall, home of his beloved mediaeval philosophy department since the late eighteenth century, a cluster of gargantuan females, all with sunglasses straddled across the top of their heads, emerged clutching plastic water bottles and cellphones and, hippo-like, waddled towards their waiting beaux.

The Arabs strode purposefully into the pack; the blacks, feigning disinterest, waited nonchalantly slack-limbed, while the Indians lingered hopefully on the edge of the merging groups, ready to pick up any residual dregs among the elephantine figures who were now greeting their escorts with cries of delight. For these lumbering Junos were students from one of the university's much-vaunted new disciplines, the Department of Rubenesque Studies.

When, some months later, Professor Trout would complain about this nightly mating ritual outside his study he was to be firmly rebuffed by the new Vice-Chancellor: "Oh, come now, Professor. It's one of the many unexpected but socially enriching outcomes of the modern university's multi-national campus. The fact that some of our foreign male students have a penchant for larger ladies has been a blessing, not only for those ladies but more particularly for this university. We already have over 200 new enrolments registered for Rubenesque Studies degrees next year and I am reliably informed much of that success is attributable to this curious appetite of our foreign male students. I gather our own British Arabic, Indian and black students, and those from America and the Caribbean, have preferences in the feminine form more aligned with our own."

Professor Trout complained about the ghetto-blaster.

The Vice-Chancellor frowned. "Yes. There have been some comments from other quarters about that, I confess, Professor. But we must be tolerant. Our new Department of Rastafarian Studies shows considerable promise and is already exceeding its budgeted student enrolments. I'm afraid any criticism of the Rastafarians will be seen as racist and then we will all be in trouble."

But to Professor Trout, a classicist to the core, and therefore ill-equipped to cope with the new order in university education and this alien taste in feminine appeal and music, his words were lost.

CHAPTER TWO

NO SINGLE EVENT marked the corruption which befell traditional university scholarship by the onset of the twenty-first century, for the despoliation had been a gradually spreading cancer over the previous four decades.

Older observers claimed the rot began half a century earlier with the advent of the pretend sciences of psychology and sociology, substituting data-gathering for scholarship and introducing a new breed of students, high in opinion and low in intellect.

In turn this had led to even more nonsensical degree courses of the education and business studies ilk, tailored to those non-intellectual students of dimmer personas, and so the floodgates of mediocrity were opened. Degrees and diplomas in media studies, folk-dancing, grief counselling, marketing, photography, cco-dynamism, holocaust studies, landscape gardening, air-hostessing: the subjects were boundless so long as a student enrolment response eventuated. All flourished in the new non-academic university environment.

Having abandoned their traditional function as promoters of knowledge, enquiry and scholarship, the universities' subsequent amalgamation with polytechnics, plus the government's ambition for every citizen, no matter how mean of intelligence or devoid of desire, to acquire a university degree, were inevitable consequences of the degradation process, and consistent with the late-twentieth-century global trend of commercialism replacing professionalism in every activity. By the turn of the century a university degree no longer commanded respect, instead becoming little more than an attendance certificate.

But much of this had escaped the attention of Professor Trout, absorbed in his mediaeval philosophy scholarship and largely oblivious to the outside world. Thus his first full awareness of the new order was firmly etched in his memory – 4.35pm on Friday the 5th of May – when he had received, personally delivered by the Vice-Chancellor's secretary, a letter advising him of the new arrangements for Anselm Hall.

He had read the letter four times, passing from mystification to disbelief, followed by horror then finally outrage, resulting in his untypical and unannounced storming into the Vice-Chancellor's office. This was all the more surprising given that Professor Trout had hitherto not met the new Vice-Chancellor. He had, however, read of his appointment in the university newspaper a year earlier, at the time with a mixture of disinterest and puzzlement.

His disinterest lay in custom, for in 37 years on the university's teaching staff, beginning as a junior lecturer at the age of 26, he had rarely met any of the university's six Vice-Chancellors who had preceded the new appointee.

His puzzlement stemmed from reading the biographical account of the new Vice-Chancellor who, selected by the University Council on the basis of his hard-headed reputation, had come to the position in late middle age without any conventional academic background. The new appointee, it transpired, had engaged in a highly successful company receivership practice, for which activity he had acquired the sobriquet "The Bristol Butcher" arising from his ruthless approach to the disposal of assets and personnel. This infamy had led to a more socially elevated career as an executive director of a prominent merchant bank, in which role he had become a favoured financial commentator by the news media, and he had readily adopted the nomenclature of the City in his utterances.

"I view a university like any other enterprise," the new Vice-Chancellor was quoted as saying in the university newspaper. "Its success lies in pro-active pruning of continually emerging dead wood to ensure a sound financial foundation and incentivise the many window-of-opportunity challenges, frequently outside the box, of the new cutting-edge competitive environment going forward."

To Professor Trout, imbued in a lifetime of correct English usage and unfamiliar with the financial world's clichéd gibberish, all of this had been mystifying. He had reread the account and, failing to discern its meaning, lost interest, wrongly assuming it all to be newspaper misprints. Oh poor fool he when so many warning bells were tolling.

But the Vice-Chancellor's letter he received a year later, advising that the mediaeval philosophy library in Anselm Hall was required for the new Department of Rubenesque Studies, was certainly plain enough and struck at the very core of Professor Trout's being.

For half a century earlier, just as England was beginning to stir from its soporific post-war years and the middle class was discovering the pleasures of public dissent, the Professor, then a shy youth, had enrolled at Ralston to pursue a history degree. In the new climate of tentative rebellion, beards were grown to convey altruistic concern, idealistic social engineering collectivism was acclaimed and angry young men emerged, their anger inflamed by the absence of clear targets for their wrath.

Restrained by a natural reticence but in sympathy with this new spirit of non-conformity, young Trout had nominated psychology as one of his degree's supplementary units. The professor guiding his course choices, having seen it all before, wisely said nothing, instead steering him towards a unit in mediaeval philosophy as a balancing factor.

Two months passed before young Trout discovered the mediaeval history library. On entering the two-centuries-old stone building he had been instantly seduced by the mellow oak ceiling panels and shelving, the leather-bound volumes, the club-like scattered armchairs and the ambience of scholarship and contemplation. This discovery had been a near-religious experience for the student, who intuitively felt that spiritually he had come home. The following year he reluctantly abandoned history and, with no reluctance, psychology, and switched his major subject to mediaeval philosophy, culminating five years later in a doctorate and his appointment as a junior lecturer.

Over the years the Ralston mediaeval philosophy library increasingly evolved as his personal sanctuary. He grew to treasure its cloistered serenity and frequently, having chosen a volume, would repair to his favourite armchair where within minutes he would be cast back into the twelfth century as a contemplative monastic scholar, a practice he encouraged his senior students to emulate. In line with this detached academic role, as time passed the Professor developed an increasingly mannered old-fashioned courtesy, in contrast to the changing practices of most of his teaching colleagues. As they abandoned suits, first for jackets and slacks and then tie-less, and ultimately in many cases for blue denim, the Professor travelled in the opposite direction, switching to tweed, and in latter years, to unfashionable three-piece waistcoated suits. When his colleagues began addressing their pupils by their Christian names or as "mate" and were addressed by them in like manner, Professor Trout maintained a strict formality of titular Mr or Miss prefixes. He had risen largely unnoticed beyond his immediate classical academic circles to his professorial status, an insignificant figure in a now insignificant department of an insignificant university. If he was noticed at all, his slight, silver-haired and neat appearance and his reactive, non-assertive manner would have him readily perceived as a pharmacist or perhaps a butler. His was a world of certainties, albeit steeped in the past, which he savoured in all of its manifestations; but now, on receipt of the new Vice-Chancellor's letter, this blissful life-long existence was threatened.

"Really Professor!" the Vice-Chancellor had scolded when Professor Trout burst into his office. "This won't do at all. It's 5 o'clock. My wife and I have a dinner engagement and I still have Frewen, the Professor of Panelbeating, to see. He's due now. Matter of fact, I thought you must be him. An unfortunate matter, all too common these days with so many of our new disciplines' staff lacking any conventional educational credentials. Frankly, C.V. checking has become rather meaningless. Still, hopefully we can place Frewen in a different field more suited to whatever talents he may possess. Apparently he was previously a journalist so – notwithstanding one's natural reservations about that – even if he hasn't coped with panelbeating he should manage with one of the less technically precise subjects. We shall see. But I'm afraid I must ask you to leave. Come back on Monday morning at 11 and we'll discuss your concerns then."

Ignoring the Vice-Chancellor's dismissal, Professor Trout dropped his letter on the desk. "This is sacrilege! It's utterly preposterous. The Ralston mediaeval library is world-renowned. Where precisely are you proposing to place it?"

The Vice-Chancellor shifted awkwardly. "Well, for the time being it will go into storage. Naturally, should opportunity arise and we can accommodate it, then we can consider the matter afresh. But regrettably, with the pressing space demands from our many new disciplines, rehousing your library is well down the pecking order of our priorities. Anyway, we'll talk about it on Monday," and he rose to indicate the termination of the meeting.

But Professor Trout, abandoning for the moment a lifetime of courteous acquiescence, untypically persisted. "Wait! You say you need the library for something called Rubenesque Studies. What on earth is that?"

The Vice-Chancellor reached behind his desk, opened a drawer and withdrew a brochure. "Here you are. This will explain everything. Now I'm sorry, but you really must leave." He rose from his desk and, stepping forward, placed an arm round Professor Trout's back, directing him firmly out to the reception area where a shifty-eyed middle-aged man wearing a shabby unpressed jacket and with the doughy, furtive face of the life-long sponger, lurked edgily.

"Ah: Professor Frewen I presume? Come in, come in," the Vice-Chancellor boomed as he ushered the Professor of Panelbeating into his office, leaving Professor Trout abandoned in the reception area.

Bewildered by this cataclysmic disturbance to his hitherto hermetic existence, Professor Trout trudged downcast back to his study, poured himself a sherry and studied the brochure.

The familiar line-drawing of the university's ivy-covered main building was on the front, and across the top Department of Rubenesque Studies was printed in embossed lettering.

Inside, the Professor read the Introduction:

> The Department of Rubenesque Studies, an affiliate of the Women's Studies School, is a progressive new intellectual discipline. Its predominant thrust is to explore the multitude of social and economic forces in western society which have conspired to achieve a manipulation of the female figure contrary to that intended by nature.
>
> The Department offers both one-year diploma and three-year degree courses and adopts flexible entry criteria with liberal cross-crediting of past academic and non-academic endeavours.

With increasing bewilderment Professor Trout read of the diverse study topics: "natural physiology, the Amazonian tradition, the genius of Rubens, endomorphic elegance, corsetry oppression, heart-failure mythology, exercise tyranny…" The list of courses continued, all totally perplexing to a philosophy scholar unfamiliar with the brave new education world of designer degrees.

CHAPTER THREE

OVER THE 22 YEARS of his former company receiver-ship career the new Vice-Chancellor had laid off a total of 338,521 employees and, believing unquestioningly that they all shared culpability for his various creditor employers' financial losses, had thoroughly enjoyed doing so. Had it not been for the advent of widespread prosperity in the 1990s he would never have entered the academic world, for he harboured a private ambition to achieve the magic figure of 500,000 sackings. But the on-going economic boom and resulting fall-off in company failures saw him reluctantly abandon this goal as unattainable.

In announcing his mass dismissals he had especially relished dealing with trade-union leaders, for holding all the cards, he rejoiced in the unionists' impotence. Suggestions of staff cuts, early retirement proposals, wage-reduction offers – he happily batted all aside, for early in his career he had learnt two golden rules, namely uncompromising rigidity and blaming others. Additionally, he had developed a repertoire of disarming debating strategies, a favourite being to deliberately confuse the names of his protagonists.

"You must understand that I am merely the mouthpiece for the creditors and am simply following orders," he had blissfully uttered many hundreds of times, and he brought these well-developed skills into his new university role.

"You must understand I am merely the mouthpiece for the University Council and am simply following orders," he said blithely to Professor Trout when they met on Monday morning.

"As I recall, that was the excuse proffered at Nuremberg – but they hanged them regardless," the Professor quietly replied.

The Vice-Chancellor was momentarily perplexed. "Nuremberg? I'm afraid I don't understand," and being a man of commerce and therefore brutishly ignorant of most things outside that narrow world, he genuinely did not.

"Never mind," Professor Trout said. "But tell me: surely the University Council appreciates the significance of the Ralston mediaeval philosophy library? They must be aware of its reputation as one of the finest in the world. You cannot just shift those treasures about willy-nilly. Our twelfth-century Folio bibles and fourteenth-century Psalter collection require the most delicate handling. Doesn't the Council realise how valuable they are?"

"Oh yes indeed," the Vice-Chancellor replied eagerly. "I

can most certainly assure you of that. Believe me, the Council is fully alert to your library's worth – so much so they have had it valued by Sothebys. If their estimate is correct, we could build four new lecture theatres from the sale of your library and also house our proposed line-dancing and installation-art departments. Both are significant window-of-opportunity growth disciplines going forward. More particularly, in pioneering degree courses in these exciting new endeavours Ralston will be first off the block and thereby effectively create a monopoly. I see no logic in persevering with the traditional disciplines, especially your sort of thing, and engaging in unnecessary competition with our rivals. Currently, as you are possibly aware, Professor Bass, the Rubenesque Studies Department is crushed into the Anselm Hall annex, where the students are literally bulging at the seams. As it stands we can just manage this year by expanding them into your library space, but this can only be viewed as a stop-gap measure. You must realise that at some point in the near future, given the rapid enlargement of the Rubenesque Studies folk, we will almost certainly require the rest of Anselm Hall."

"And us? The mediaeval philosophy department?" Professor Trout demanded.

"Well … naturally that's a matter we'll deal with when it arises," the Vice-Chancellor said cagily. "But let me be frank, Professor: you're 63. Presumably you're not intending to carry on indefinitely."

This remark struck a chord with Professor Trout. Only a week earlier he had read a newspaper article claiming that the biggest killer was not cancer or pneumonia but retirement. He had thought a great deal about this since, and more or less resolved to continue what he was happiest doing: specifically, being Professor of Mediaeval Philosophy at Ralston.

"This is preposterous!" he exclaimed. "The Ralston Mediaeval Philosophy Department is internationally recognized as a leader in its field. Are you not aware that its existence is the very reason this university was founded?"

"You may be assured the University Council has taken that into consideration," the Vice-Chancellor responded breezily. "But I remind you again, Professor Salmon: I'm merely following orders and those instructions are … how shall I put it … not encouraging outlook-wise going forward for your department. You see, the problem the Council has in respect of your department's doubtless fine reputation, is that at this point in time, no-one – the wider public that is – actually cares. If they did – well, let's face it, you would have a considerably larger number of students."

"My name is Trout; and I'm sorry, Vice-Chancellor: I don't see your point."

"Trout, Trout you say. Please forgive me, but regardless, Professor Trout, you have a mere 31 students yet in addition to yourself you enjoy two lecturers, two secretarial staff and three librarians and occupy some of the university's finest premises. Cost-wise, it's a most unsatisfactory one-to-four staff/student ratio. I am of course merely following orders and those orders going forward are to achieve a minimum one-to-twenty ratio in all departments. In those circumstances it strikes me your pending retirement provides a window of opportunity for the university to rationalise the situation."

"And what will become of my staff?" Professor Trout demanded angrily.

"That, I'm pleased to say, is not a problem, at least with your lecturers. The librarians pose a dilemma for which I see no ready solution given the Council's visionary objective to ultimately achieve a bookless university. The wonders of our technological age can only be marvelled at, don't you agree Professor?"

"No," Professor Trout responded but the Vice-Chancellor, now in full flight, ignored him and continued: "Your lecturers, well, I'm happy to say they will not be wasted. Most of our new disciplines require merely supervisory skills rather than any particular subject expertise. Your staff will simply have a change of topic, to ... as it were, more progressive fields relevant to the real world. For example, our new Academy of Installation Art currently requires two tutors and your lecturers may be eminently suited to fill those positions. It would be helpful if you were to consider Professor Frewen, whom you encountered last Friday evening. He is an excellent example of the new academic flexibility the University Council seeks going forward. Perhaps he was overly ambitious in accepting the panelbeating professorial role on the credentials of 40 years of motoring – doubtless a few dents over that period conceded, but incurring them is one thing; repairing them's another, as Professor Frewen discovered. Nevertheless, we've been able to deal with that difficulty very satisfactorily. Professor Frewen accepted a junior lecturer's position in the Rubenesque Studies Department, which is a far more suitable role given, as it transpires, his excellent credentials, so from this week he's to become a neighbour of yours. Apparently his wife is, as it were, a larger lady so he has appropriate practical experience for his new field of scholarship; and we do need male staff in that department. Hopefully it will help attract male students to fulfil its optimum growth potential going forward."

"I read your brochure," Professor Trout said, now furious at this proposed disruption to the formerly placid rhythm of his life. "From what I can ascertain, this Rubenesque Studies thing is targeted at fat girls with the single objective of assuring them it's all right to be obese."

"A harsh observation, Professor Kipper," the Vice-Chancellor responded curtly.

Ignoring the insult, Professor Trout snapped, "Well, if that's not the case, what is it about?"

The Vice-Chancellor thought for a few moments. "Well, to some extent, viewed narrowly as it were, in the perspective of a casual and may I say, a glib viewpoint, what you have said is on face value correct. It's simply not the way we like to put it."

"Oh? So how do you like to put it?"

"We consider the more intangible wider benefits, Professor, particularly in the context of the march of progress going forward."

"Such as?"

"First and foremost, from the university's viewpoint

Rubenesque Studies is a very popular course, which takes us to the nub of the issue: specifically, if it's popular then it's profitable. And being a profitable academic discipline, until we can introduce the necessary curricular reforms, it carries those which are unprofitable – perhaps best epitomised by your own, Professor," the Vice-Chancellor concluded smugly.

"Yes, that may well be so. But I was unaware of any obligation to view mediaeval philosophy scholarship as a commercial activity," Professor Trout retorted angrily. "Tell me," he added after an awkward lull had ensued. "You say the benefits of this Rubenesque thing are many. Aside from your ... your profit concerns," he snorted, not hiding his contempt, "what others are there?"

"Ah," the Vice-Chancellor said contentedly. "Now you're talking. Let me state the position clearly. The modern university is a broad church and no longer an elitist monopoly for a privileged minority to indulge in what many now view as esoteric irrelevancies. The modern university caters to all, tailoring its courses to fit its students' interests and aptitudes. You refer – somewhat unkindly if I may say – to fat girls..."

"That's because they are – all of them – grossly obese," the Professor snapped. "I have the misfortune to view them every day."

"Well, be that as it may, let me remind you, Professor, that larger-proportioned ladies are entitled to consideration in their educational needs every bit as much as anyone else. And fiscally, given their rapid expansion – I refer to the department, not the students – their contribution to this institution is not to be lightly dismissed. You are perhaps unaware, Professor, that a third of all Americans are now clinically obese. As is so often sadly the case, we Britons trail the Americans but the trend is positive and I have no doubt we will attain a similar situation in the near future."

"Surely obesity is a health issue?" the Professor insisted. "I would have thought it was a matter for doctors or dieticians, or even psychologists."

"That is an old-fashioned outlook, Professor. The Ralston progressive approach is entirely in accord with the new thinking which does not view corpulence as an abnormality: indeed, given current trends it will soon become the norm. Anticipating that, as we have done with our Rubenesque Studies degree, places us firmly in the vanguard of the modern approach. That aside, we can proudly boast that a degree in Rubenesque Studies sends those young women out into the world with a sizeable sense of self-worth rather than ..."

"Equipped for what?" Professor Trout interrupted.

"A question one may well ask of your mediaeval philosophy students, Professor," the Vice-Chancellor responded silkily, all his well-honed combative skills from his previous careers coming into play.

"I could answer that," Professor Trout said, "but I rather fear it would be pointless given your hint of closing down my department altogether."

"Not a hint, Professor, not a hint: a reality. Your department will close itself down. I've been studying the records. Forty years ago there were over 200 mediaeval philosophy students, admittedly in most cases only as part of a humanities degree majoring in something else. Nevertheless it's been a declining trend ever since. Obviously if you could find a sponsor then we might take a different approach."

"A sponsor?"

"Yes, of course. It's the modern way. A corporation to fund a Chair. Half a million pounds, I suggest, would quickly terminate any division in our respective outlooks. Consider Rubenesque Studies. The Chair in fact is the Kentucky Fried Chair of Rubenesque Studies. Furthermore, the sponsor has offered another £50,000 a year if we allow them to build one of their facilities on campus – preferably near the Rubenesque Studies Department. Fortunately there's an excellent site available adjacent to Anselm Hall. That lawn is a disgraceful waste, given the space pressure on us. Their proposal goes before the next University Council meeting – I might add with my strong recommendation."

The Vice-Chancellor rose. "I've enjoyed our little discussion, Professor, but now I'm afraid you must excuse me. I have a meeting with our new air-hostessing professor. Now there's an example for you. They've secured a £1 million endowment from Singapore Airlines to fund their Chair," and he ushered the very confused Professor Trout from his office.

CHAPTER FOUR

ROFESSOR TROUT REREAD the concluding para-
graphs of Theopopolus's draft thesis with mixed
feelings. The American's quibbling at seminars was infuriating
but there could be no doubt about his brilliance. The work
was first-rate; indeed it was deserving of publication in book
form and the Professor felt a glow of pride at his pupil's
scholarship.

Theopopolus's well-argued assertion that the influence
of Grosseteste in thirteenth-century thought was massively
overrated, because it was largely derivative, would certainly throw
a cat among the mediaeval philosophy pigeons. The Professor
chuckled in anticipation of McCairn's indignant reaction at
Harvard; and as for Rankin at St Andrews and the boisterous
Professor Ponz in Munich, they would be outraged at the heresy
and certainly have plenty to say. The attractive prospect of the
inevitable stimulating rumpus in philosophy journals resolved

Professor Trout to visit Walter King, publisher at the University Press, first thing in the morning, although he would make it clear that publication of Theopopolus must follow his own opus, now finally completed after fourteen years' work. King had been pressing him in recent weeks for the manuscript to ensure its inclusion in the forthcoming end-of-year book list. Perhaps, the Professor reflected, he should wait before proposing publication of Theopopolus, at least until after his own comparatively uncontentious work had exhausted its potential for reviews in philosophy journals. His manuscript, entitled *The Absence of Radicalism in Mediaeval Philosophic Evolvement*, was intended as an erudite study for advanced scholars, its primary thesis lying in a speculative explanation for the gradualism characterising the evolvement of mediaeval philosophy.

The Professor weighed the idea of having a small party at home to celebrate publication. His wife Enid could probably handle the catering if there were only six or eight guests. On the other hand, all things considered, perhaps he should run to a larger gathering at the university, he mused. Damn it all, after fourteen years of hard grind he deserved it; and he began to mentally tot up a guest list, only to be disturbed in this pleasant contemplation by a hesitant tap on his door.

"Come in," he called, annoyed at the interruption. The door tentatively opened and the Professor recognised the abject figure of Frewen, the new junior lecturer in Rubenesque Studies, who entered and stood twitching nervously before him, his mere presence striking a discordant note in the book-lined study.

Professor Trout's face darkened. "Mr Frewen, I believe," he barked uncharacteristically, not hiding his distaste.

"I'm … s… s… sorry to bother you, Professor," Frewen stammered. "I wonder if I might have a word."

"Might, might; what do you mean 'might'? Either you will, as you put it, 'have a word', or you will not. It is not an issue of 'might' but one of fact, and uncertainty on the issue is a matter entirely in your hands and therefore inappropriate to raise with me."

Frewen seemed to visibly freeze under this barrage – his lips quivered and for a fleeting moment he appeared on the verge of flight.

"Well?" the Professor demanded.

Frewen shifted edgily, his eyes flitting about the study. "I'm awfully sorry, Professor, but I've been sent to convey a concern. She made me do it," he whimpered.

"Who made you do what? What are you going on about?"

"The Head of the Rubenesque Studies Department – Professor Beefenstein. Between you and me, Professor, she can be a bit of a Nazi – but you probably know that."

Professor Trout did not know that; nor did he know the Beefenstein woman, but since the Rubenesque Studies department had shifted into Anselm Hall he had occasionally observed a prodigious red-faced creature of barely discernible gender who always wore a doctoral gown and looked about to explode. This bovine creature he presumed must be Professor Beefenstein.

"Well? You say you have a concern. What is it? We don't

have time to waste in this department," clearly implying the opposite to be the case with Frewen's activities.

"It's the smoking, Professor. Your pipe, that is. Some of the Rubenesque Studies students have complained about you smoking at the open window. They say it's threatening their health. Silly, of course, but the Professor made me take it up with you – a man-to-man chat, she said. I didn't want to, but like I said, she's a bit Hitlerish and I can't afford to get offside, so here I am."

Professor Trout stared at his visitor, astonished. "Are you intoxicated, Frewen?"

"I wish I was," Frewen muttered unhappily. "I'm just doing what I was told."

"Health concerns," the Professor erupted, his voice rising. "Health concerns! Are you mad? Those grotesques you're encouraging must have damned limited life expectancies, a state of affairs entirely self-inflicted, and you accuse me of threatening their health. Is this some sort of joke?"

"Please understand, Professor. I didn't want to come. To be honest, my career's on the line. Not the smoking matter," Frewen added quickly. "Just generally staying onside with everyone. I never thought I'd crack it in academia and it's been a life-saver, to tell the truth. Nothing else has been much good for me before."

Professor Trout reached for his pipe, stuffed it with tobacco, lit it, drew heavily and blew smoke towards his visitor.

"A lovely aroma, Professor," Frewen said unctuously. "I often wished I could smoke a pipe."

"So what stopped you?"

"Well, the expense actually. Probably sounds silly but the pipes and tobacco and all the rest of it – might as well have cost millions from my perspective. Never could really put my finger on it but somehow I seem to have always been broke. Different now though – at least so far, fingers crossed – since I've landed up in the academic world with a regular salary coming in. Maybe I should consider a pipe now," he added thoughtfully.

"Isn't that somewhat inconsistent with your purpose in coming here?" Professor Trout suggested.

"Oh Lord, you're right," Frewen muttered. "God, I'm a goose. You can see why my previous jobs always ended on a bit of a low note," he added amiably.

"I assume, that being the case, they must have enjoyed some corresponding high points," Professor Trout teased, but Frewen, a life-long recipient of scorn, was oblivious to his mocking tone.

"Oh yes. It's not always been disastrous. Just seems to end up that way – you know – in the poo."

"I gather you were formerly a journalist," Professor Trout said.

"Yes, yes, I was," Frewen responded eagerly to this rare show of interest from another human being.

"Any high points?"

"Well … there was one time I was in line for a deputy editorship. Only a small paper, mind – a freebie in fact, in Yorkshire. Anyway, I didn't actually get it, and after that ended in the poo I came south and had quite a few jobs with different papers and magazines. Once I even had a weekly column. Only for two weeks though," he added ruefully, and then brightening, "Still, that's journalism for you: up one day and down the next."

"So how did you end up here?" Professor Trout asked, conscious of a growing, almost ghoulish interest in his pitiful visitor.

"Ah," Frewen declared. "That was certainly my lucky break. After the last sacking I was running my eye over the job ads and lo and behold, there it was. I tell you, Professor, as soon as I saw it, something deep inside told me that this time my ship had come in. See, the university was advertising for a professor for its new panelbeating department and the advert went on about organizing and writing abilities and that sort of general stuff and hardly mentioned panelbeating, so I thought, nothing ventured, nothing gained and banged in an application. Best thing I ever did."

"Oh? How's that?" Professor Trout asked, gesturing Frewen to a seat, his curiosity now fully aroused.

"When I met the appointments committee they were terribly pleased. Never had that before with a job interview. Usually with newspapers it's trial periods and warnings and a fairly unwelcoming tone, but this time it was just the opposite. All the other applicants were panelbeaters and the appointments committee were most unhappy about that. Quite the wrong image for the university, they said, and rightly so too. You may not know this, Professor, but panelbeating's the bottom of the heap in the motor trade and mostly done by criminal types."

"No, I can't say I knew that," Professor Trout said, willing Frewen on.

"Well, not being used to such a nice reception I got a bit carried away and told the committee that if accepted I would write a history of panelbeating. That made them very excited. Seems there's never been a book written on the subject. It would become the standard textbook worldwide, they said, so I was appointed on the spot. See, Professor, the name of the department was the Department of Applied Panelbeating and as they said, it lowered the tone for the university not having any theoretical side to it. So, hand-in-hand with my appointment, the name was shortened to the Department of Panelbeating Studies.

"First day on the job I was taken to meet a chap called Dr King. Don't know if you've heard of him: he runs the University Press. They print books, Professor. Well, that was a bit of a let-down I can tell you. Everyone had been so nice up until then but King was extremely cool; matter of fact I won't pull my punches, Professor: he was downright rude and discouraging. Quite uncalled for, if you ask me. I see no need for it. It was just like being back in journalism. Everyone being rude all the time and looking down their noses at us."

Walter King and Professor Trout were life-long friends and, conscious of his colleague's respect for scholarship and his intolerance of anything less than the highest academic standards, the Professor was filled with anticipation. "So what happened next?" he asked.

"I tried to be friendly," Frewen grumbled. "I told Dr King I always felt I had a book in me, but instead of encouragement which is what a chap might expect, he said, 'Let us hope it stays there.' Damned short-sighted attitude if you ask me: after all, where would King be if it wasn't for authors like me beavering away writing books?"

"Where indeed?" Professor Trout said agreeably, for listening to Frewen's rambling discourse his initial curiosity had now evolved into unabashed fascination. The thought struck him that befriending Frewen could be useful. He would have a spy in the enemy's camp, which was how he now viewed the encroaching Rubenesque Studies Department. To the Professor, the Rubenesque absurdity represented barbaric hordes threatening civilization. He was determined to resist and Frewen could be a useful Trojan horse as a first step. "Perhaps you'll join me in a sherry?" he suggested.

Frewen's eyes lit up. "I say, Professor. That's rather decent of you," and Professor Trout rose, opened the cabinet behind his desk and brought forth the sherry bottle and two glasses.

"So, Mr Frewen, how did you arrive next door?"

"Usual story," Frewen muttered confidingly. "Can't say I was surprised at the time as it all seemed too good to be true – the panelbeating job that is."

"The poo again," Professor Trout suggested helpfully.

"'Fraid so. Thing was, I made a point of staying clear of the panelbeating workshop. Apart from not being able to offer much, not knowing anything about it like, we already had two retired panelbeaters as tutors, although they were actually called lecturers, and they seemed to have everything in hand – and anyway, I have a strong aversion to noise. So I thought, I'll show that King chap up, and I got stuck in doing the textbook. Problem was what to write. I mean panelbeating's a modern thing which has only arisen with widespread car ownership and to be truthful, it was hard to find what to say, there not being any books on it to copy from. Then I had a brainwave. It struck me that the roots of the industry basically lay with mediaeval armorers – you know, your sort of stuff, making suits of armour and swords and things – so I jollied about in the university library until one of the librarians found a book for me with a few references to all of that. I copied them all out then wrote a fair bit about the history of the motor-car – plenty of books on that to copy from – and after three months I had knocked together what I thought was a damned good effort. Then I took it to Dr King at the University Press."

"Yes, yes," said Professor Trout, riveted by Frewen's appalling vulgarity. "And what did Walter … Dr King that is … what did he say?"

Frewen shook his head slowly. "The poo again," he said sadly. "Still, I don't see how that excuses rudeness. No call for it, I say."

"What happened?" the Professor asked eagerly.

"Dr King read the first two pages then flicked through the rest, then he told me to follow him. We went outside and do you know what? He put my manuscript on the ground then – you won't believe this – he set fire to it and danced about it waving his arms and whooping. Not the sort of behaviour you'd expect from someone in his position."

"Yes – go on. What did you do?" Professor Trout begged, enthralled by this account.

"Well, you see, it was my only copy so I told him he should consider himself very lucky that I'm a peaceful chap. If I wasn't I might have punched him," Frewen said peevishly.

"Yes, yes, tell me more."

"Well, King looked at me in a very menacing manner, I can tell you, and he said, 'Frewen, if you were to punch me you would make me the happiest man in the land for I would then feel free to reciprocate.'" Frewen paused and thought for a moment. "Don't you find that peculiar? Personally, I put it down to professional jealousy. What do you suppose it all meant?"

"I have no idea," the Professor said, scarcely able to hide his delight. "So what happened after that?"

"Next thing I had a call asking me to see the Vice-Chancellor. Here we go I thought: the poo again, but instead I was transferred here. At first I was puzzled, as panelbeating and Rubenesque Studies seemed a bit different, but once the Vice-Chancellor explained it, it seemed to make sense. As he said, from an intellectual standpoint, the two disciplines had an obvious empathy in their shared respect – he actually said reverence – for a fundamental natural form, if you get my drift Professor."

This was too much for Professor Trout. "No," he said emphatically. "No, I do not get your drift, Mr Frewen. Please elaborate."

"Oh well, no matter: I never really understood myself. There was a pretty big salary drop going from being a professor to a junior lecturer, which was a let-down, but the important thing is I'm still here. In a spiritual sense I feel I've arrived: you know, come home to my true destiny in academia, so my main concern now's to stay out of the poo."

Professor Trout seized his opportunity. "I see," he said. "Perhaps as an old hand I can be of assistance with poo-avoidance. I want you to feel free to call in for a sherry and a chat occasionally, about five."

"I say!" Frewen exclaimed, but he was lost for further words and with puppy-dog eyes he looked at the Professor, overwhelmed with gratitude.

CHAPTER FIVE

ISPLAYING THE JOURNALIST's well-developed mag-
neticism towards free alcohol, Frewen required no
repetition of Professor Trout's invitation and two or three times
a week he arrived at the Professor's study around five. Sherries
were poured and in response to probing and encouragement,
Frewen revealed a past of spectacular ineptitude and serial
disasters, an unimaginable existence to the Professor which
held him spell-bound. Soon the Professor found himself
voyeuristically looking forward to the visits as an amusing
end to his day.

Of greater value and as hoped, Frewen proved to be a
source of information, not only about the Department of
Rubenesque Studies, but of other worrying developments in
the university, mainly learnt from his eavesdropping.

Once, the Professor's spirits rose when Frewen reported
alarm in the Rubenesque Studies department at the mounting

loss of fat girls through many being whisked off to Africa by their beaux. "Seems being fat and white they're considered trophy brides back in the jungle," Frewen explained, shaking his head in disbelief. "No accounting for the darkie mind, Professor."

But the optimism this news induced proved short-lived, for a few weeks later Frewen advised that the department was back in growth mode. Encouraged by the Vice-Chancellor, Professor Beefenstein had conducted an intensive promotional campaign in Germany, resulting in a flood of fat fraulein enrolments.

Frewen's own teaching activities as a junior lecturer were also a source of wonderment to Professor Trout.

"Found it a bit tricky at first," Frewen conceded. "I kicked off handling the heart-failure mythology and anti-exercise courses. Had to do a bit of research on the heart-failure stuff until I finally learnt the ropes – you know Professor: you've been at it longer than me."

"The ropes? Sorry: you'll have to explain."

"Tricks of the teaching trade: that sort of stuff. Soon got the hang of it. Basically I discovered I just have to rant for a couple of minutes; doesn't really matter what I say, then I throw the floor open for discussion and the fat girls do the rest. Usually we run out of time. They're all real keen to tell stories about skinny uncles who died of heart attacks and friends who've come a cropper in gyms or through dieting, and I just listen till the session's up. Lecturing's a breeze now."

"Are you telling me all of your classes are conducted in this fashion?" Professor Trout enquired, not hiding his bewilderment.

"No, no, Professor. We don't have classes. Professor Beefenstein says classes reflect teacher-pupil social oppression stemming from historic contrived male superiority. What we have instead are workshops."

"But this is a university degree course! I assume you at least have exams?" Professor Trout asked.

"Good Lord Professor, we don't have exams. To be honest, I thought they'd ended everywhere. I actually asked Professor Beefenstein about exams myself when I was still a bit green, and she ear-bashed me for quarter of an hour. Claimed they're the ultimate male oppression. Being still a new chum I kept my trap shut – you know, not letting on I wasn't up with the play; poo avoidance-wise. Mind you, as it's our policy to pass all the students, it does seem silly to make the fat girls sit exams."

"So … there's no essays or tests of any kind?" the Professor pressed.

Frewen's face screwed up in annoyance. "That's a worry, I don't mind telling you. We still have essays. They're the one black spot in my academic vocation. Personally I can't understand the point, seeing everyone gets to pass. But bloody Beefy insists on one a week though."

"Well, I'm afraid you'll just have to grin and bear it," the Professor said conciliatorily. "Marking essays is certainly time-consuming but there's no escaping their value in advancing scholarship."

"No, no: wrong end of the stick," Frewen exclaimed. "Marking's not the problem. Anything over 8 pages I give an A, 6 to 8 pages a B plus, 4 to 6 pages a B and anything less gets a C. I make them number their pages and can rip through marking the lot inside two minutes. My record so far is one minute and 23 seconds. I time the marking as a personal intellectual exercise – you know, to keep the old mind sharp. No: as I said, marking's a breeze; it's the bloody topics that's the worry. See, I've got to think 'em up. It's all very well for the old hands who've been on the job for a while, but the way I see it, it's damned unfair for new chaps like me. It's been quite a strain, I can tell you."

This difficulty was resolved a few weeks later when Frewen arrived one evening in high spirits.

"Ah, the pleasures of the world of scholarship, Professor. S'pose more than anything the great advantage of being an intellectual is when a problem arises, one can put the old thinking-cap on and find the answer. Solved the essay-topic dilemma," he announced proudly.

"Oh? How have you handled it?"

"Ever noticed a specially large fat girl, Professor? Always wears orange-and-black-striped leotards. My pick is she'd come in at a stripped fighting weight of over 350 pounds. You can't miss her."

Professor Trout nodded. The particular grotesque had been awesomely conspicuous owing to her preposterous body-fitting attire, in contrast to the other fat girls who mostly wore athletic track suits and running shoes, without irony.

"Sharlene bloody Crudd," Frewen declared. "Only daughter of a Cardiff pastry-cook. He sends her a whacking great carton of meat pies every week. I've just cut a deal with her. She's going to think up the essay topics and in return I'll give her an A – or record an A, more like. The deal is she doesn't have to write any essays herself. 'Cause of that she's chucking her courses in Apologetic Studies and's now gunna major in Rubenesque Studies, even though it's harder. Doesn't matter being more difficult, seeing as I'm passing her on everything."

"Apologetic Studies?" the Professor exclaimed. "What on earth is that?"

"New this year, Prof. One of our Rubenesque Studies lecturers applied for the professor's job. I heard her moaning to old Beefy about it. Seems she was the front-runner but lost out to a dwarf because the appointments panel said Ralston was under-represented with disabled staff."

"But what is it? This Apologetic Studies thing you mentioned."

"You know, Prof. Apologising for being white and not black and European and not a wog or for not being a lesbian or a paraplegic – that sort of stuff. Big new field 'pparently, with lots of counsellor jobs going with town councils. Lotta our Rubenesque Studies fat girls are doing units in it. Anyway, the main thing is old Sharlene Crudd's dropped it, which takes care of my essay-topic problem. A satisfactory outcome all round, what?"

Professor Trout did not respond to this observation. "So what exactly do you do all day, between conducting your lecture sessions?" he asked.

"Fixed that problem. I bought a telly and watch the game

shows and soaps. Quite an expert on them now, I am." Frewen cast his eyes about the room. "I see you don't have a telly Prof. You're welcome to come and watch with me anytime you want. Helps to pass the time, I can tell you."

On another occasion Frewen arrived dejected. It transpired he had been allocated field study supervision for the forthcoming new term.

"Field studies?" Professor Trout queried, bracing himself for a fresh preposterous revelation.

"Misleading title," Frewen grumbled. "There's no study involved. It's entirely protest stuff. Beefy's given me a list of places I have to lead protest rallies to. Bloody embarrassing, I can tell you."

"I don't understand," Professor Trout said.

"We're hiring a bus and I'm to escort 40 fat girls at a time to demonstrate outside places. You know: gymnasiums, airlines and cinemas and chair manufacturers to complain about small seats, clothing manufacturers, the Health Ministry to object to their anti-obesity campaigns, Weight Watchers and Jenny Craig head offices, modelling agencies, beauty contests: that sort of thing. Seats are the big one, of course. Particularly nasty about seat issues, the fat girls are, and they go on about it all the time. Matta fact Beefy's planning a new course called Seating Conspiracies. She reckons it's all a deliberate plot to humiliate women. Seems lots of the fat girls have sat on seats which have collapsed under them – that's when they can fit into them."

"Can I assume then, that your lecture room seats are larger than normal?" the Professor enquired.

"Not just larger, Prof. Steel-reinforced and padded. Bloody important too, as I've noticed Beefy and the fat girls hate standing up. They dive for seats at the first opportunity. Anyway, now I've got to lead these protests. For the past week we've all been flat out painting abusive signs."

"I'm sure you could slip quietly into the background while the demonstration is going on," the Professor said encouragingly.

"Like hell! Bloody Beefenstein's ordered me to get arrested. Break a window or knock a policeman's helmet off or something like that, she says. Claims it's part of the intellectual protest tradition and will be good publicity for the department. I'm not happy about it, I can tell you. I can see it leading to the poo again."

Once Frewen entered looking intensely solemn. "I say, Professor," he enquired. "Would you mind giving me some advice, you know, from one scholar to another?"

"What's on your mind?" Professor Trout asked.

"I've been thinking," Frewen said edgily, then hesitated, plainly reluctant to elaborate further.

"Come now Mr Frewen," Professor Trout urged, anxious for the inevitable titillation arising from every Frewenian revelation.

"Well," Frewen said cautiously. "Basically ..." he paused again, then abruptly blurted, "I'm considering growing a beard. Haven't resolved the matter yet, mind, but the thing is, I thought it might help convey a more scholarly look. I'd very much value your opinion," and he gazed at the Professor searchingly.

Struggling to maintain a sober demeanour Professor Trout replied solemnly, "Mr Frewen, I believe that is a first-rate proposal. You absolutely must have a beard," and for half an hour he engaged in an immensely enjoyable discussion as to the appropriate hirsute mode. Frewen, atypically, sought moderation in a trim, moustacheless look. The Professor urged a full Victorian-era style and in support produced pictures of Marx and Trollope. Eventually he prevailed with his clinching statement: "Mr Frewen. A staff member with a beard like that would be unsackable." This assertion required no confirming argument, for the mere hint of employment permanence seemed sufficient to convince Frewen.

It was agreed for tidiness' sake that commencing the beard would be deferred to the next term break, but in the interim under Professor Trout's enthusiastic guidance, the task began of achieving a scholarly image through other devices. As instructed, Frewen purchased three second-hand tweed jackets at the town's Saturday flea-market.

"It is essential they have a battered look to achieve the appropriate intellectual flavour," the Professor explained, and on his advice Frewen took the jackets to a tailor to have leather patches sewn on the elbows.

"I say, Professor," Frewen complained the following evening. "The tailor said leather elbow-patches are out of date."

"Precisely," Professor Trout declared. "Exactly the right image. It will testify to your having your mind on higher matters rather than the fickle transience of fashion." He additionally instructed Frewen to acquire four pairs of different-coloured corduroy trousers, half a dozen different-hued turtle-necked jerseys, a pipe to sit in his jacket pocket and horn-rimmed spectacles with plain lenses.

A difficulty arose when the Professor proposed the permanent adornment of a book under his arm. "Change it daily," he advised. "No-one will be able to see the title so ensure, for example, that a large blue book is followed by, say, a small red one to convey the impression of rapid consumption. Anything from your personal library will do."

"But I don't have any books," Frewen observed, an announcement which initially stunned the Professor. For a few seconds he was lost for words.

"You see," Frewen explained, "books have never really been my forté; not in the reading-of-them sense, that is." He pondered for a moment then added, "Price of a busy life, I suppose, not having time to have read one." He looked about the book-lined study. "You've got lots in here, Professor. Hadn't really noticed them before. Read any of them?"

"Most of them, Mr Frewen; most of them, I imagine," the befuddled Professor muttered.

"Mmm," Frewen said thoughtfully. "Maybe I should get one. I'll give it some thought. Anything in particular you'd recommend?"

Rather than respond, the Professor abandoned the book idea and instead, to add a slight touch of the academic eccentric, advised Frewen to always wear a red beret, even indoors, and tilted slightly to one side to provide a hint of the cavalier. "It will become your signature mark and convey the sense of an open mind able to embrace all intellectual viewpoints and issues," Professor Trout told Frewen. Additionally, he coached him with practice sessions in his study towards achieving an intellectual gravitas, this involving Frewen walking up and down slowly, frowning at the ground and muttering aloud to himself. This latter touch, the Professor realized, was particularly important although he refrained from explaining why. A mumbling, shuffling figure would deter conversational overtures from students and staff alike and act as insurance against exposure.

Within a few weeks the make-over was completed. The Professor took pride in his creation, for there was no doubt Frewen now projected the thoughtful and vaguely eccentric donnish look he had sought to achieve without succumbing to questionable bohemian pretensions.

A few weeks later Frewen arrived in a pensive mood. "I say Professor," he said. "You ever been abroad?"

"Abroad?"

"Yes – you know – overseas: wogs, gyppos, frogs – all that shower."

"Why, of course! What an extraordinary question!"

Frewen appeared hurt by this response. "Not every chap has," he muttered. "Personally, I've never quite found the time. Price of a busy life I suppose." He brightened. "Mind you, I went to Belfast once – job interview – didn't get it. Not sure if Belfast properly counts as abroad, does it?"

"No," Professor Trout said adamantly. "It most certainly

does not. But why are you raising this?"

"Ah, yes," Frewen said, snapping out of the reverie his Belfast memories had induced. "I'm going abroad. I've applied for a passport," he declared proudly.

"What? You're leaving your Rubenesque Studies career?" the Professor exclaimed, dismayed.

"No, no, of course not! The thing is, that's what I'm hoping you can help with. Beefy's taking me with her to a place called Clone. You heard of it?"

"Clone? It's in Ireland, I believe."

"No, that can't be right. Beefy says it's in Germany."

"Clone?" The Professor thought for a moment. "Do you perhaps mean Cologne?"

"That's it! Heard of it, have you?"

"Yes," Professor Trout muttered weakly. "I've heard of Cologne."

"Can't say I have," Frewen said ruefully. "Mind you, geography's never really been my forté. But it's OK is it? I mean, you know what one hears about these dago places. Quite safe, do you think?"

"Yes, Mr Frewen. I think you will have no cause for alarm in Cologne. But why are you going there?"

"It's an international Women's Studies conference with delegates coming from all over the world. Your advice on the tweed jacket and spectacles and beret is what did it. Old Beefy's treated me quite decently ever since I bought all that intellectual clobber. About bloody time, too. When I first arrived she was pretty damned cool to me, I can tell you.

Same with the other lecturers. Upset at having a bloke on the scene, if you get my drift. Different now though, specially since I started wearing the beret. But here's the snag. Being pioneers in the field we're supposed to explain Rubenesque Studies. Beefy's giving a paper and's told me I must also, to add weight to the overall presentation. Thing is, I've never done – you know – written a paper and given a speech. I'm worrying myself sick about it."

"When is the conference?" the Professor asked.

"This August, so I've still got two months to prepare," Frewen said. "Might as well be in two minutes' time or two years for all that it matters," he added glumly. "I'm still not gunna come up with anything so I was wondering like, if you think you could help – not delivering the speech of course," he added hurriedly. "Appreciate I'm gunna have to handle that myself. Writing the paper's the problem. To be honest I was never much good at writing. Not really my forté, if you know what I mean."

"But you were a journalist!" the Professor protested.

"Yes, well, that's the thing you see," Frewen said sheepishly. "Mostly I could sort of manage – for a time anyway, if they'd just give me a chance but, well, that's what usually led to the poo with the bloody editors. I tell you Professor, editors can be damned unreasonable. Stay well clear of them: that's my advice."

"I see. I'll bear that in mind. But what I don't understand is how you think I can help with your paper. Have you a topic?"

"Beefy's given me that," Frewen grumbled. "I have to talk about the role of Rubenesque Studies in the twenty-first century. A bit bloody rich, if you ask me. I mean, what would I know about it?"

Professor Trout thought for a moment. With his book now finished he was already feeling the itch of writing withdrawal symptoms. Throughout his career he had attended numerous philosophy conferences and delivered papers, all in the scheme of things now rather pointless, he reflected. 'Philosophy and the New Millennium', 'Responsible Philosophy', 'Philosophy and the Contemporary World', 'Philosophy in a Materialist Age', 'The Philosopher's Burden' … all grandiose sounding; so many addresses, so many conferences; so, so silly. As an old hand he certainly knew the procedure. Keep the addresses short – begin and end with a joke, make a single point and use lots of big words in between. Everyone, he realized, loved attending conferences, especially abroad. But he was sufficiently a realist to recognize that the pleasure lay solely in holidaying at someone else's expense, and the single drawback was having to actually attend the sessions and listen to speeches. Whether the speakers spoke gobbledegook or erudite wisdom was irrelevant. Both were a pain for the audience, and the addresses, once delivered, were instantly forgotten. In the circumstances the prospect of writing Frewen's paper was enticing.

"Perhaps I can help," he said, and Frewen's eyes lit up. "Bring me some Women's Studies textbooks and I'll put something together for you."

Frewen became visibly emotional. "I say Professor, you're a life-saver," he stumbled, and then, "You know what I really respect about being a scholar – apart from all the paid holidays, that is. It's the fraternity. Chaps helping chaps. I can tell you, it was never like that in journalism. Law of the jungle there. Quite different altogether. Chaps knifing chaps in the back all the time." Overcome, he produced a grubby handkerchief and noisily blew his nose. When this trumpeting finally ceased and he had stuffed the handkerchief back in his pocket, he said solemnly, "I tell you, Professor, I've got a very strong feeling, you know, down here," and he patted his stomach, "that somehow I've found my true vocation in academia and getting in the poo will become a thing of the past."

"Let us hope so; let us hope so," Professor Trout said encouragingly, barely able to hide his delight.

The following evening Frewen returned carrying a plastic bag from which he triumphantly withdrew a bottle and with a flourish, placed it on the Professor's desk.

"Appreciate all your help, Prof. A small gesture of thanks," he said proudly.

Professor Trout examined the label, which bore a luridly coloured illustration of two red-cheeked and beaming peasants seated at a crude wooden plank table and toasting each other with glasses aloft. The inscription read Finess Pure Sherie – Product of the Republic of Moldova.

"Well," Professor Trout exclaimed, "I'm touched. But where on earth did you find it?"

"Ah. Now that's a story," Frewen said mysteriously.

"Yes. I'm sure," the Professor said, eyeing the label suspiciously.

"Say no more, Prof. Say no more," Frewen said, tapping

the side of his nose with an extended finger.

The Professor rose and produced the corkscrew.

"No, no, Prof. Not necessary. It's a screw-top."

Professor Trout poured two glasses and took a tentative sip, then he spluttered and spat into his handkerchief. "Forgive me," he muttered, eyes streaming. "I'm afraid I'm a bit off-colour today. I appreciate the gesture but" – this to Frewen's visible relief – "there's really no need. The university supplies its senior academic staff with sherry," he lied.

Once on a rain-sodden day Frewen arrived carrying a plastic water bottle and wearing sunglasses astride his beret. The Professor was appalled and reprimanded him.

"Beefy and the fat girls all have them," Frewen explained. "Even inside the workshop rooms. I thought I should too: you know, Prof, empathising and all that stuff, if you get my drift."

"No, no, no," Professor Trout complained. "Quite the wrong image altogether. You will undo all my good work with this preposterous nonsense. You are a scholar, an intellectual, a thinker. Your students will want to look up to you as someone special, someone above the common herd, a learned man of the world steeped in knowledge and free of mindless behaviour."

Thereafter Frewen abandoned the plastic water bottle and sunglasses-on-top-of-the-head empathy strategy.

On another occasion Professor Trout suggested to Frewen that he acquire a lady's bicycle, preferably with a wicker basket at the front. Noting Frewen's alarm, the Professor retreated a little.

"It's not so much the bicycle that's important," he explained. "More the bicycle-clips round your trousers – just the right image."

"Don't quite get your drift," Frewen complained. "Appreciate your advice, but you can't expect me to ride about with my head down mumbling. Won't work. I could crash into things. Anyway, Prof; funny thing I know, but I never had a bike – don't know how to ride one. Price of a busy life I suppose," and that proposal was also abandoned.

As the months passed, while still maintaining a certain formal distance, Professor Trout became increasingly forthright in his interrogations. Attempts at ascertaining Frewen's home background encountered resistance. There were mumbling references to "my Gran" but otherwise Frewen was untypically reticent about his upbringing. He was, however, more forthcoming about his career history. A watch-repairing apprenticeship had lasted a week and had been followed by a rat-catcher trainee job. "Didn't really have the brains for that one," Frewen freely volunteered. Thereafter a series of menial and always short-lived employments had occurred before he had finally landed a position as a junior reporter. "Much more me," Frewen explained. "Felt instantly at home in journalism. Chaps all like myself – on the same wavelength if you get my drift, Prof."

But despite these revelations he maintained a persistent aloofness about his family and eventually the Professor decided not to press the issue, realizing that to know everything about Frewen would end his curiosity, and with it the pleasure he was deriving from the tidbits of banality. One issue, however, weighed on his mind and one evening he braved the matter.

"Your junior lectureship," he said, choosing his words carefully, "I gather you were able to secure the position based on first-hand … as it were, practical experience – on the home-front, if you take my meaning."

Frewen looked blank, plainly uncomprehending. The Professor pressed on. "Your wife," he blurted. "I understand she is, as it were," he hesitated … "a larger lady."

"Oh. Gotcha now," Frewen said, relaxing. He lowered his voice conspiratorially. "Tell the truth Prof, she's not actually my wife, not in the sense of being married if you get my drift."

"I see. So you're still the gay bachelor," the Professor said lightly, relieved that Frewen was not offended at this line of questioning.

Frewen contorted his face. "No, no, I'm not a poofter Professor. Don't know why you should think that. But funny thing, now you mention it, I'm not a bachelor either. To be honest I completely forgot. The thing is, I was married once. Still am, I s'pose. She was an Irish waitress up in Sheffield. Bit of a slag actually, all things considered. What happened was I got a job on the paper there, met her on my second day, married her a week later" – this announced in a tone of accomplishment – "got in the poo, so the following week headed south and I've never seen her since. Strange really, getting married like that when you think about it. Still, you know what it's like, Prof. When a chap's got a few drinks aboard anything can happen."

Professor Trout did not know what it was like having a few

drinks aboard and as a consequence marrying an Irish slag, but he refrained from saying so. He had been married to Enid for 37 years and had an adult son and daughter, both now pursuing successful careers after completing their university educations. "So your current, ah ... friend. How did you meet her?" he probed.

"Lucky break," Frewen replied. "Thing was, I was really deep in the poo at the time. I'd come to London to apply for a job. Speech-writer for the boss of some outfit called the World Trade Organization." He became pensive. "Don't know about you, Professor, but I see no need for rudeness. Had an appointment at 4.30pm and found myself booted into the street five minutes later. I was actually interviewed by the head banana. Fellow called Moore. An Australian I think. What he said to me ... no ... I can't tell you. I'm a peaceful man, Professor, but I tell you I was damned close, believe me, damned close to taking a poke at Moore. Told him so too. Know what? He laughed and invited me to go ahead. Not the sort of behaviour you'd expect from someone in his ..."

"Yes, yes," Professor Trout interrupted impatiently. "But what about your wife ... ah, your lady friend that is?"

"Oh yes. Well, afterwards I found myself wandering down Piccadilly. Felt pretty damned low after being threatened with violence like that, I can tell you. Still, like they say, every cloud has a silver lining. Suddenly I heard a shout, 'False Start' and ..."

"Falstaff?" Professor Trout quizzed.

Frewen looked sheepish. "No, Prof. 'False Start'," he emphasized. Bit of a nickname I had up north with the other chaps. Anyway, lo and behold there was bloody old Bert Cooper. He'd been on the Leeds *Gazette* when I'd a stint there about three years earlier. 'Come and have a drink and meet the fiancée,' he said. Lucky bugger had fallen on his feet and landed a job with the *Daily Mirror*, so having nothing to do, off I went with him. Well the fiancée came in; not a bad looker either, and with her was her mate, this bloody great fat girl, well – woman really, I suppose. She was a bit long in the tooth; hitting 40 actually. Turned out she was a high-powered executive type. After about an hour Bert said come to dinner so off we all went, one thing led to another, and being broke and having nowhere to go at the time I ended up shifting in with the fat lady. Lovely flat in Knightsbridge; saved my life I can tell you." Frewen lapsed into a thoughtful silence.

Elated by this account, Professor Trout dared not break into his reverie and waited patiently. After a minute's reflection, Frewen continued. "To be absolutely honest I can't say it's all a bed of roses. I mean speaking man to man, you know, in those circumstances there's obligations on a chap which at first I found a bit terrifying, with her being so enormous. But basically we've sort of slotted into an understanding – down to once a week, if you get my drift. I've found with three or four whiskeys under my belt and in the dark, I can get by, as it were. Get it over and done with's been my policy, then there's a week's peace and quiet. But like I said, it's not exactly perfect. Take my beer mat collection. Got it nicely mounted on display placards but she won't let me hang thcm up. Her home, of course, still I can't say there's not times when I look at other chaps' wives and girlfriends and feel a bit short-changed."

"So … living with this lady was a sufficient credential for your new position?" the Professor pressed carefully.

"That's why I really can't complain, all things considered," Frewen acknowledged grudgingly. "Would never have landed the job otherwise. See, first the Vice-Chancellor offered me a job as an Installation Art tutor. Made a silly blunder I did, and let on I didn't know what it was. But then the Vice-Chancellor grilled me about my background and once he heard about my partner he offered me Rubenesque Studies. Actually he was most supportive. He launched into a pretty fierce attack on some of you chaps – heads in the clouds, ivory towers, all that sort of stuff. Told me one lesson he'd learnt from life was to never underestimate the value of practical hands-on experience, and he said in that respect I was ideally suited for Rubenesque Studies, so here I am. All's well that ends well."

As the months passed the information mounted, although the Professor learnt nothing from Frewen which offered an opportunity to counter-attack the Rubenesque Studies territorial threat. Probing into Professor Beefenstein's doctorate had proved unfruitful. She had gained it in Women's Studies from the University of Los Angeles.

More disturbing was the news that Professor Beefenstein was working on a Rubenesque Studies textbook to be published by the University Press. Professor Trout felt for his friend Walter King, knowing how distasteful this would be to him.

"Wouldn't have minded a crack at it myself," Frewen conceded ruefully. "The royalties could be very useful. When

I suggested it, bloody Beefy got quite nasty so I pulled the old head in smartly. Poo avoidance," he added in explanation.

"Matta fact that reminds me of something I was going to ask you about, Prof. Beefy was talking to this old university mate of hers over from America last week. She's a feminist vegetarianism professor in California. Anyway, they were sitting at the table next to mine in the caf so I thought it could be smart to listen in and see if I could pick up a few clues about getting on in academia. Cut a long story short, this feminist vegetarian prof said she'd just had her ninth book published, all in the last five years. Then Beefy went on about all the books she was planning to knock out. Thing was, I got a strong feeling from what they were saying that the more books you bring out, the safer your job is. You reckon there's anything in it, Prof?"

"An astute observation, Mr Frewen. It is indeed a generally accepted maxim that being published consolidates one's academic position," Professor Trout replied.

Frewen pursed his lips and became thoughtful. After a few moments lost in contemplation he said ruefully, "Damn pity about King burning my panelbeating manuscript, then. Maybe I should redo it seeing as I know all the stuff to copy out from. Whatta you reckon, Prof?"

"I'm not altogether sure that would enhance your reputation as a Rubenesque Studies scholar," the Professor replied, and when Frewen looked perplexed he added, "It's a different subject, you see."

"Oh right; gotcha Prof," Frewen exclaimed. "You mean I'd

have to write one about Rubenesque Studies for it to help?" Alarm spread across his face as the implications of this burden sank in.

"That is the standard procedure, I'm afraid."

Frewen looked downcast. "See, the snag with that, Prof, is I think the old Beefenstein wants to keep it all to herself. Like I said, she cut up real ugly when I said I was going to knock out a Rubenesque Studies textbook myself."

"Perhaps you could write a pamphlet on one of your courses. That would still qualify for inclusion in your bibliography," Professor Trout suggested.

"Don't quite get your drift, Prof."

"If I recollect rightly you mentioned you were lecturing in heart failure mythology. If you were to write a small primer on that topic then it would certainly go on your book credit list."

"No Prof. Not lecturing. I conduct workshops. Problem is though, what if they don't like what I write? You know, the University Press. Might not publish it."

Professor Trout weighed this consideration. "I think you can relax on that count, Mr Frewen. In your broad social science area I understand it is the fact of publication rather than content that counts most."

"Gotcha, Prof. Respect for scholarship you mean?"

"Not exactly that. Perhaps one might say respect for effort."

Frewen screwed his face up. "Difficulty is, Prof, I don't really know much about it. I just leave it to the fat girls to carry on under their own steam."

"I see your dilemma," Professor Trout said. He thought for a moment. "Can I suggest you confine the next few essay topics to it. Doubtless your students will produce sufficient heart-attack mythology material to utilise for your pamphlet."

Frewen's face lit up. "My God, Professor, that's brilliant. I'll get on to it smartly." He looked around the book-lined study. "You write many of these, Prof?"

"None, I'm afraid. However, my first book will be published shortly."

"Just one, Prof; well you do surprise me. Still I s'pose there's not much you can say about your field and once someone's done a book on it then you're basically stuffed – right? Not like Rubenesque Studies. Being brand new, it's wide open. Also, a lot more to it than your business. Once you've covered joisting on horseback then it's basically all wrapped up." Suddenly his face darkened. "Tell you what though. This time I'll have a word first with the Vice-Chancellor. Get him to sort that King fellow out in case he burns it again."

Concern crossed the Professor's face. "There is another option, Mr Frewen. You could keep a copy of your manuscript."

Again Frewen brightened. "You're a genius, Prof. Would never have occurred to me. See, in journalism we didn't do copies of our stuff."

"No, I don't suppose you did," Professor Trout said magnanimously. "The important thing is there's no need to mention Dr King to the Vice-Chancellor," and to reinforce the point he rose and topped up Frewen's glass.

CHAPTER SIX

S IT TRANSPIRED, the Vice-Chancellor had already talked with Dr King about his publishing policies, for the following morning on arrival at his study, Professor Trout found his friend waiting to see him.

"I'm the bearer of terrible news," King said. "The Vice-Chancellor's pulled the plug on your book. Not just yours either: my entire end-of-year list. It's unbelievable! He claims he's just following orders from the University Council. Apparently they've insisted that everything published henceforth must make a profit within three months of publication, which is quite ridiculous. I tried explaining the role of a university press and how it all works but he just kept moronically chanting about following orders. So I'm shifting to Scotland. I knew old Hamish McDonald, the St Andrews University Press publisher, was retiring at the end of the year so I called him, the position was still open, I flew up for an interview and I'm to take over. Handed in my resignation last night. Didn't tell you earlier because I thought I might talk the Vice-Chancellor round once I told him I was leaving, but it made no difference I'm afraid. To be honest he seemed quite pleased about my going. Frankly I have serious doubts about his sanity. At our first meeting he kept calling me Dr Prince and then yesterday it was Dr Duke."

Once more Professor Trout found himself running through the gamut of emotions, again culminating in his storming into the Vice-Chancellor's office.

"Well, I'm sorry Professor but my instructions from the University Council are unequivocal," the Vice-Chancellor said briskly, plainly annoyed by Professor Trout's intrusion. "Rationalize every activity in the university going forward. That's my brief, and that's what I shall do. We have a warehouse overflowing with academic books we've published, now simply gathering dust. Frankly, they're pure self-indulgence – mostly, I might say," he emphasized, "products of the humanities faculty. The mere fact of their unwanted existence is proof they should never have been published, so tell me Professor: who will buy your book?"

Professor Trout, fighting to protect fourteen years of devoted scholarship, began a stumbling explanation. He listed the many university philosophy departments and journals worldwide and insisted that over the years the copies would gradually feed out.

"Not good enough, I'm sorry," the Vice-Chancellor said triumphantly. "While that jammed warehouse doesn't give one cause for optimism despite your assurances on future sales, what you're failing to budget for are the holding costs. I'll let you into a secret, Professor. The warehouse won't even exist in another year. Our architects have drawn up plans to replace the brick infill side panels with windows and the building is to be utilized for our planned one-year cake-decorating diploma course, for which preliminary market research suggests a considerable student demand. We intend to move with the times, Professor."

"This is preposterous!" Professor Trout protested. "Regardless of my years of work writing my book, you can't possibly close down the University Press. It's a fundamental part of every university's …"

"Who said anything about closing it?" the Vice-Chancellor interrupted. "We have no intention of doing so, at least not at this point in time. Instead we're bringing it into line with the new century's values. No more books people don't want. There's absolutely no logic in that. From now on we're only publishing books people actually buy, and not just buy but snap up as soon as they're printed."

"Such as?" Professor Trout demanded.

"Councillor Gwyther summed it up very well, I thought. Being a prominent sharebroker he brings to the University Council considerable commercial acumen. As you know he's soon to become Chancellor and I'm looking forward immensely to working with him. A sensible, pragmatic man capable of thinking outside the square, which is exactly what is required. Matter of fact, it was he who persuaded me to accept this office. In respect of the University Press he has provided a single guideline going forward – 'the riot control police'."

"Riot control police? I don't understand," Professor Trout said, confused.

"Well perhaps he doesn't mean it literally," the Vice-Chancellor reluctantly conceded. "Rather, it's an aspiration he suggested we must always aim for. Henceforth book publishing is to be confined to titles which, on release, hopefully require the riot control police outside bookshops to hold back the crowds of eager buyers. Without such lofty goals going forward, greatness for this higher learning institution will never be achieved."

"That's absurd!" Professor Trout exclaimed. "Utterly absurd. The very essence of a book is contemplative. You're treating it like an everyday commodity … like … like a Harrods sale. It's simply not how books work."

"Absolute rubbish, Professor Fillet," the Vice-Chancellor exploded. "Good Lord, man, I've seen it with my own eyes. Once in Manchester I witnessed dozens of policemen outside a bookshop restraining huge crowds and diverting traffic. That was the Spice Girls book, if I recollect rightly. Same thing another time in Glasgow. Couldn't get near the mall, the crowds were so dense outside W.H. Smith's when a Princess Di book was released. Made me late for my appointment. And come to think of it, I was in Birmingham when that footballer fellow – what's his name – English captain as I recall … there must have been 3,000 people there. Those are the sort of books we must publish: proper books, books people actually want, not books they self-evidently do not."

"So you won't publish mine, then?" Professor Trout demanded.

"Of course we will, Professor Kipper," the Vice-Chancellor said soothingly. "But only subject to your convincing me it will pass the riot control test. Anything else would be a dereliction of my duty. I can't say fairer than that. Perhaps you could tell me what your book is about."

Encouraged by this invitation, Professor Trout endeavoured to explain, but in the face of the Vice-Chancellor's unblinking stare he soon found himself floundering awkwardly. Eventually the Vice-Chancellor interrupted.

"I find myself in a quandary Professor. Frankly, I'm at a loss to understand why anyone today – that is five hundred or one thousand years or whatever – your field – you know how many years later – should care a whit about the pace of absorption of new mediaeval thinking; and furthermore, I don't believe anyone does. With the greatest respect, I do not believe your book will satisfy Councillor Gwyther's riot-control test."

With a sinking heart Professor Trout began another clumsy justification about the virtues of scholarship, but the Vice-Chancellor held his palms up to stop him.

"Please forgive my intrusion, Professor, but there's one small matter niggling at me. Precisely what is the appropriate pace for new thinking to be adopted? Is there an established standard? Indeed, I assume there must be if you use the relative term 'slow'. So you see, I'm left wondering, slow compared with what? Perhaps you could explain."

Professor Trout could not. In desperation he submerged his anger and resorted to diplomacy. "I really think you should reconsider, Vice-Chancellor. The issue is not black and white. As John Ruskin said, there are two kinds of books: those of the hour and those for all time."

"Who?"

"Ruskin."

"Can't say I've met him. One of your staff, is he? No, Professor Herring. I'm afraid it's no good appealing to me. I'm only following orders."

For Professor Trout this was war, and the time had come for action.

CHAPTER SEVEN

"GENTLEMEN, GENTLEMEN, PLEASE, this simply will not do," Professor Trout, as meeting convener, rose and appealed from the stage, then becoming conscious of 22 female academics glaring at him, he added, "And ladies." Slowly the noise subsided.

The Professor resumed his seat and continued. "I strongly urge that we now abandon this line of discussion. We are in agreement, after all, so I suggest it would be more fruitful to direct our thinking to an appropriate strategy."

A reluctant murmuring of dissatisfaction arose from the 62 Humanities faculty professors and lecturers present, of whom many remained unsated in tendering their recriminatory anecdotal accounts. The meeting had already run nearly two hours as, to sympathetic cries of outrage, speaker after speaker indignantly described horror experiences from the steadfast encroachment on their floor space and resources by the multitude of newly introduced, purported fields of study.

Periodic attempts by Professor Trout to short-circuit the complaints and progress the meeting had been frustrated, as if the purpose of the assembly was solely to vent disgruntlement rather than explore practical ameliorative measures. Not for the first time the thought crossed the Professor's mind that there was something innately unpragmatic in his Humanities colleagues' approach to life: that they seemed childishly naïve in their faith in mere protestation to put things right whenever they believed they occupied the high moral ground.

Alert to the practical difficulties of conducting a meaningful meeting should too many attend, Professor Trout had initially intended confining it to senior professors of the established non-nonsensical disciplines. But he had been obliged to reconsider this strategy following his encounter with the notoriously crusty Dean of the Science faculty, the 72-year-old biologist Professor John Bayley.

"Wasting your time appealing to me," Professor Bayley snapped. "We've had nothing but co-operation from the new Vice-Chancellor. The Science faculty has expanded faster in the two years he's been on the job than at any time in the last forty."

"How can you say that, given he's closed the astronomy department and replaced it with astrology?" Professor Trout demanded.

"Oh, make no mistake, I was angry about that at the time. Took it up with him too. But I could hardly object when he reminded me the astronomy department had only five students; and closing it, among other things, is what funded the general expansion of the sciences, which I repeat, has been considerable." He hesitated and became pensive. "You know, we scientists endeavour to explain the world, to unlock its secrets as it were …"

"We philosophers attempt the same," Professor Trout interrupted.

"Perhaps, perhaps," Professor Bayley said sharply. "But as a scientist I'd rather take the short route and actually look into a horse's mouth to see how many teeth it has; not sit around so-called philosophizing trying to work out the answer. In that sense the Vice-Chancellor is very much in our camp. When I protested about the astrology outrage he pointed out how many famous people actually rely on that nonsense. He even claimed Reagan consulted an astrologer. I'd always assumed it was just housewives and homosexuals. I'm a biologist, thank God, but if I were a behaviourist I might try and explain this irrational conduct. Nevertheless, I suspect you won't find too many leaders consulting philosophers, specially the most powerful like Reagan; or, for that matter, Hitler or Genghis Khan."

"Then you're wrong," Professor Trout said. "Genghis Khan certainly did. Why, once when confronted with a problem he sent a delegation of warriors all the way to southern China to bring back a famous philosopher he'd heard about so as to present the issue to him. The whole exercise took two years, as Genghis Khan was in northern India at the time."

"I see. And did this so-called famous philosopher solve the puzzle?" the Science Dean sneered.

"That's not the point. The important thing is that even someone as barbaric as Genghis Khan valued philosophers."

"Simple superstition," the Science Dean snapped. "Totally pointless if to no avail. Whatever the problem, I suspect a scientific approach would have been more fruitful. Am I right? Did your famous Chinese so-called philosopher come up with the answer?"

Professor Trout shuffled awkwardly. "Unfortunately he never really got the chance. By the time he reached northern India Genghis Khan had forgotten what he wanted to ask him. But you can hardly blame the philosopher for that. However, I'm merely observing that you're wrong about Genghis Khan and philosophers. Philosophy is not something vague and mystical, which is why I'm so surprised to find a scientist endorsing astrology."

Professor Bayley was visibly angered. "I'm doing nothing of the sort," he barked. "The closure of the astronomy department had nothing to do with the introduction of that rubbish other than the coincidence of timing."

"It's a corruption of the university and everything it stands for," Professor Trout persisted. "As a scientist you should be at the forefront of objectors, which is essentially what our meeting is about. Along with all the other ridiculous new courses, it destroys any vestige of a university's image as an institution of higher thought and scholarship. A university should be something the public look up to, and respect; and without putting too fine a point on it, the conscience of the nation."

"Corruption of the university!" Professor Bayley exploded.

"It was you lot in the humanities who started the downward spiral, allowing sociology and suchlike in without protest. Fifty years ago university degrees commanded automatic respect. Now they're mostly a joke. But there's still one exception and that's a science degree. It's even more meaningful today than before."

"I take your point," Professor Trout conceded, "but that status still applies to humanities degrees in the traditional disciplines."

"Does it? Are you sure of that? Let me tell you something," the Dean said, measuring his words carefully. "This university's been my life. I came here when I was 17, finished my doctorate when I was 25, and have been on the teaching staff ever since."

"The same for me," Professor Trout intervened agreeably, but the Science Dean ignored him and continued in the same stern manner.

"When I was a fresh-faced junior lecturer I looked up to humanities scholars as the apogee of intellectual life. In those days, 50 years ago, before all the silliness started, it was you historians and philosophers and Shakespeareans and so on whom we scientists all regarded with a fair degree of awe as scholars and – what was it you called it? – ah, yes: the conscience of the nation.

"I don't mind admitting that back then, in my innocence and keen to advance my own thinking, I literally cultivated you people. But did I encounter scintillating intellectual debate in the staff room, at dinner parties or anywhere else? No, I did not. To the contrary. I encountered arrogance and sloth and words, words, words – everyone babbling and no-one listening. Just a flood of clever-speak verbiage flowing out to well-deserved obscurity."

"I'm sure it wasn't that bad," Professor Trout interjected, but the Dean was not to be stopped.

"It was worse. Almost without exception I found intellectual laziness in the mindless, unquestioning acceptance of obviously flawed, left-wing ideology, contrary to all social and economic evidence, and in a destructive, envy-based prejudice against successful people, particularly in politics and commerce. As a scientist with a mindset pitched towards understanding cause and effect, I blame the post-war Labour governments. Unlike today's Labour politicians they were then mainly made up of ambitious trade unionists, and those types were imbued with ideas and philosophizing and placed you humanities academics on a pedestal. They viewed us scientists with disdain because they considered us merely an advanced form of what they were escaping from. We were practical people, lacking in their eyes any lofty intellectual flavour, and so we became stigmatized, resulting in a disastrous fall-off in science and mathematics students. Instead, everyone aspired to your humanities know-allism and then onwards to pontificating careers with the BBC and the like. Parasitical plundering of the taxpayer rather than participating in lowly trade, was what it all amounted to.

"But believe me, I tried to comprehend your stuff. What ultimately brought me to my senses was reading Hegel's *Science of Logic*. Far from offering any 'science' or 'logic' all it amounted to was nonsensical verbosity, and my growing scepticism about you humanities wafflers and philosophers turned to cynicism. It's the age-old story: once you lot no longer had to sing for your supper, the rot set in. So I abandoned your company when I realized that humanities academics, far from being the conscience of the nation as you put it, at best could merely boast of training those who are."

"What do you mean?" Professor Trout demanded.

"You humanities types have blown it. You have effectively been privatized. Nowadays all advanced thinking on the big issues of the day comes from privately funded think-tanks and higher journalism. It certainly doesn't emerge from humanities faculties as it did before the war."

"Thank you for hearing me, but obviously I'm wasting my time," Professor Trout said unhappily, stung by the rebuke he intuitively sensed might be partly justified. He rose, but at the door stopped. "You know, you should still be with us, if only to protest at the astrology outrage."

"Ah, but I don't think it's an outrage," the Science Dean said smugly. "Of course it demeans the university, but as a practical man I now accept the Vice-Chancellor's approach. As he pointed out, it's the social misfits and losers attending that foolishness and the other rubbish courses he's introduced who have provided the funding increment for the real and worthwhile endeavours. And as he also said, if those idiots didn't do it here, you may be assured they would somewhere else, so we might as well have the financial benefit."

"There is where we part company," Professor Trout said coolly. "You will find it is a maxim among philosophers that the end never justifies the means."

"Which is why your lot never achieve your ends," the Dean snapped, and he turned away dismissively.

Later that day Professor Trout's friend, the eighteenth-century literature professor, Rohan Hill, elaborated on this. "When I was protesting to the Vice-Chancellor about the encroachment of this ridiculous Spiritual Drumming Department on our space he spelled it all out. He said the hard science disciplines made perfect sense to him. Same with accounting and law and commerce. 'Useful, practical activities' is how he described them. It's solely the Humanities faculty and particularly the traditional humanities disciplines that he's targeting. Sociology, Women's Studies and the lightweight, unscholarly, data-gathering things he's happy about because of their high student numbers. But with us he was most insulting and claimed we were indulging in activities which were no more than verbal games and hobbies. I tried to explain but it was like talking to a brick wall. I don't think he listens. He kept calling me Professor Mountain and when I corrected him he apologized then ten minutes later addressed me as Professor Peak. The man's a philistine, I tell you. If he knew about Socrates he'd happily prescribe a dose of hemlock for us all."

In the light of all this Professor Trout had decided to limit the meeting solely to selected humanities professors from the traditional fields, but even then he encountered opposition. The classics professor, currently Dean of Humanities, had firmly rebuffed this plan. "The professors have the standing," he conceded, "but it's not necessarily what's required. We need street-fighters, and speaking for my department I can tell you that my lecturer McNally is precisely the sort of fellow required for this exercise – a no-nonsense, go-for-the-throat Herculean type when it comes to argument. No one can beat him. I promise you: if anyone can sort the Vice-Chancellor out, he can."

Bowing to the Dean's advocacy and status Professor Trout had relented and, just as he had feared, the enlarged meeting had quickly descended into a chaotic rabble.

"May I propose a plan of action?" Professor Trout rose and appealed again. "As I've said, I see no purpose in further recounting our experiences. We're all in the same boat. We've all encountered the same problems. I propose we elect a committee to decide a course of action, and then execute it."

A welcome murmur of approval rose from the floor and, encouraged, Professor Trout plunged on. "Before inviting nominations may I also suggest, again for practical purposes, that we confine the committee to six persons."

Further consensual noises floated up to the stage whereupon, now overly confident in his chairman's authority, Professor Trout made a tactical blunder. "May I further propose that, as a sensible starting point, all present who would like to serve on that committee raise their hands." All but three promptly did so, and once again the meeting erupted.

Professor Trout blanched. "I see," he said. "That, I'm afraid, does not resolve our difficulty."

The historian Professor Munz rose. "There are eight departments present. I propose we extend the committee to eight and each department choose its own representative."

Cries of dissent arose. For another twenty minutes confusion reigned as speaker after speaker tendered solutions to the action committee membership structure crisis. Some complained at the production of an agenda without the whole meeting's approval; others insisted on an equal representation of women. A youthful English lecturer demanded at least four younger representatives to dispel any flavour of fogeyism and was promptly swamped by indignant counter-arguments from older academics about the virtues of experience, and so the meeting floundered on, although in no purposeful direction. Listening to all of this from the stage, Professor Trout began to despair of his colleagues, who were confirming in their behaviour all the criticisms made about them by the Science Dean.

Eventually the Shakespearean, Professor John Algie, rose, and in a stentorian voice bellowed, "I wish to move a motion. I move that Professor Trout, as the meeting convenor, assisted by the Dean, personally select the committee."

"Seconded," shouted Algie's senior lecturer, who was currently pursuing promotion, but the proposal was lost in a hubbub of angry protests and points of order from across the lecture theatre.

Dismayed by this turn of events, Professor Trout exercised the traditional trump card of all popular leaders under anarchical siege. Rising yet again, he held his arms aloft in a call for silence.

"I fear I have lost the confidence of the meeting," he said. "In the circumstances I shall stand down and allow you to appoint a new chairman."

It was an astute ploy which resulted in an instant uproar of protest followed by several minutes of speakers' endorsements and culminated in a standing ovation for Professor Trout who was now re-established, only with stronger authority.

A further hour achieved selection of the committee, comprising four professors and four mainly youthful lecturers, with a tidy gender divide of women and men.

The meeting broke up with a discernible mood apparent, namely that having now elected a committee, the underlying problem which had provoked the assembly was somehow resolved.

The committee met the following day in Professor Trout's study and, fearing another inconclusive rabble, this time he arrived with a plan.

"I would like to recommend that as a first step we apply the old adage of 'know thine enemy'," he said. "As I see it the best way to do this is to have an initial meeting with the Vice-Chancellor, express our general concerns, hear his responses and then we can devise a meaningful strategy." With surprising efficiency given the previous day's tumultuous gathering, the committee concurred and an appointment was duly arranged with the Vice-Chancellor.

It was not a success. In boxing parlance it was a gross mismatch for although the Vice-Chancellor was outgunned eight to one, in reality it constituted a heavyweight champion in the ring with eight flyweight novices.

For nearly an hour the Vice-Chancellor listened patiently, for he too was a practitioner of the know-thine-enemy strategy.

As a veteran of numerous such battles in his former career he knew always to box cautiously in the early rounds, probing his opponents' defences and allowing them latitude to fire their best shots before mounting his counter-attack.

Having heard out their complaints, he opened his assault with a gentle feint to lull them into a false sense of security. "First I would like to thank you all most sincerely for giving up your valuable time to outline your concerns. I strongly believe that with the right paradigm inside the loop, achieving a successful university requires a team effort, and to work well going forward, it must be a happy team with result-driven synergies to achieve a win-win situation."

The eight complainants visibly relaxed. Despite the bewildering commercial-world gibberish the Vice-Chancellor's tone suggested this was a much better response than expected. Plainly they had won him over. Noting with a practised eye his opponents' lowered guards, the Vice-Chancellor then threw a series of snappy jabs to further weaken their defences.

"A modern university is a democracy and as with all democracies there is a power structure, in the case of this institution comprising the staff and the administrators acting together in pro-active harmony under the University Council's guidelines. I'm sure I speak for us all when I say we must never betray the trust placed in us by our dependent constituents, namely our students. Is that not so?"

Lulled into a sense of security by this seemingly harmless proposition, the committee nodded their agreement.

"Excellent," the Vice-Chancellor declared. "If I might now

take this a step further. Our students are free to choose their careers. I'm sure we would not wish it any other way; that is, for us to tell an aspiring history or philosophy or classics scholar, 'No – we know best – you must become an accounting or line-dancing student'."

Appalled by such a hypothesis, the eight academics vigorously concurred; and having created his opening, the Vice-Chancellor now banged home a devastating sucker punch.

"You have complained about Rubenesque Studies, air-hostessing, lip-reading, panelbeating, astrology, flower-arranging, grief counselling and many of our other exciting new fields of scholarship which you say are encroaching on your resources. They are doing that for one elementary reason, namely that they are the academic pursuits our students are freely choosing to study. It is those courses which are exploding in student enrolments; yours, I regret, are declining. We are simply responding to our students' career decisions, a policy you have indicated in no uncertain terms you endorse. It is, my respected colleagues, nothing less than democracy in action."

A babble of protest erupted.

"Wait," the Vice-Chancellor shouted suddenly, holding up his hand. He looked at his watch, then picked up his pen, wrote something on a scrap of paper then, resorting again to a defensive waiting strategy, said, "I apologize for interrupting. Please continue."

The uproar resumed, all endeavouring to speak at once. Eventually a poetry lecturer with a piercing voice prevailed and the others reluctantly fell silent before her stridency. For ten minutes she shrilly expounded: "... academic standards ... higher values ... finer things ... intellectual rigour ... solid foundation for ... intangible ... unquantifiable ..." The Vice-Chancellor listened patiently and then, just as the lecturer reached an emotional peak and launched into an exposition about "preserving our rich cultural heritage", he leapt to his feet and delivered the knock-out punch.

"Stop!" he shouted again. Flushed with triumph, he picked up the piece of paper he had written on ten minutes earlier, then looked at his watch.

"My watch is accurate," he said to his puzzled audience. "Examine your own and I believe you will find it is exactly 4.46pm." Mystified, the academics glanced at their watches. The Vice-Chancellor held up the paper. "You will recall I wrote this ten minutes back," he gloated. "Please read it and you will observe that I have written '4.45pm – culture'," and he passed the paper across the desk.

Resuming his seat, his hands now clasped contently across his middle, he continued. "It has been my experience – an extensive experience I might add, extending over two decades and across the land dealing with redundant activities – that when those with a vested interest in their continuation without regard to the necessary subsidy falling on society for such continuation, having failed to produce any valid argument and when all other resources have been exhausted, always resort to the fall-back of 'culture'. As you have witnessed, I can usually predict to the minute when the word 'culture' will rear its head.

"In my former role as an insolvency specialist I spent twenty years closing obsolete industries in the face of vigorous opposition from self-indulgent vested interests. I have heard how ship-building, cutlery manufacturing, coal-mining, steel production, motor-cycle making and many, many other activities, all now, for the greater good of Britain, no longer part of our economy, must be preserved despite their financial burden on society; because they are part of our cultural heritage.

"Consequently you will appreciate why, when I hear the word 'culture' used in argument I steel myself, knowing I am about to endure an assertion with a single underlying proposition, namely why an activity lacking any rational economic basis should be continued for the parasitical benefit of its practitioners at the expense of everyone else. That, my respected colleagues, is what the term 'cultural tradition' means to me."

The eight academics sat in stunned silence.

The Vice-Chancellor looked at his watch again. "I have greatly enjoyed our little discussion, so much so that I'm afraid we have expended over two hours. Regrettably I must call a halt, for I have another commitment. I am obliged to say a few words of welcome at the function for two new Astrology Department lecturers, which as you are doubtless aware, is currently our third fastest growing discipline in student enrolments. Perhaps some of you were planning on attending, and if so I shall look forward to your further company there," and smiling contently he rose and left, another knock-out victory chalked up on his undefeated record.

CHAPTER EIGHT

THE PASSING OF two days after the disastrous meeting saw the action committee's rage now redirected from the offending new courses to the Vice-Chancellor. Again the committee met in Professor Trout's study.

The Professor listened resignedly to the flow of invective. "Barbarianism ... intellectual sabotage ... narrow commercialism ... cultural vandalism ... fascism ... Americanism ..." The predictable indignation was vented, but it was now tinged with a tone of despair and defeat. Very soon the protestations abated and Professor Trout resumed control.

"I have given the matter much thought, as is apparent you all have," he said. "The difficulty we face is what to do next. There seems no purpose in a further meeting with the Vice-Chancellor unless we can produce fresh arguments and, try as I might, I can't imagine what they could be. The problem we have is his persistent claim that he is only following orders."

"We'll go over his head," a classics lecturer cried. "We'll appeal directly to the University Council."

"That has occurred to me," Professor Trout responded. "Unfortunately, I rather suspect it will prove futile. I looked up the current Council membership. They're all stockbrokers and financiers and that sort of thing. I'm afraid it gave me little cause for optimism."

The Humanities Dean now spoke. "I warned you," he grumbled. "I told you we should have had McNally. He'd have handled it. He's quite impossible to argue against."

"But you selected your representative for the committee," Professor Trout reminded him brusquely.

"No disrespect to my colleagues," the Dean said, "but they were all most insistent that as Dean, I should be our delegate. I offered to stand down but …"

"Yes, yes," Professor Trout interrupted impatiently. "It really doesn't matter now. The important thing is what to do next."

"If the Dean thinks this McNally chap's so damned good why not let him have a go at the Vice-Chancellor?" Professor Munz suggested. In the absence of any alternative ideas, the action committee unhappily concurred and the meeting ended.

The Dean remained behind to discuss the McNally proposition and Professor Trout brought out the sherry.

"Ghastly fellow, McNally," the Dean explained. "He's the sort of Irishman who I understand is actually quite common, notwithstanding the more familiar buffoonish stereotype image. Not exactly the Oscar Wilde, scintillating witticisms rapscallion type either. He's a teetotaller, grimly intense, a real hairshirt devotee through and through. Never laughs, no small talk or social graces, highly intellectual in a gloomy pessimistic fashion. Dreadful company, quite dreadful. He was in a seminary for four years. The usual story: doubts and all the emotional baggage accompanying that. Eventually he saw the light, tossed it in, completed his classics doctorate, married, no kids; monstrous wife, active in the Green movement which probably explains his permanent gloom …"

"He sounds appalling," Professor Trout intruded. "I imagine he's bearded."

"Naturally, and he is appalling; make no mistake about that," the Dean replied. "The students can't stand him. As I said, not the twinkle-eyed stereotype Irishman. He's devoid of any human warmth but is still an adequate teacher: you know, gets the message across satisfactorily although he doesn't exactly wind the students up into a fervour of enthusiasm with his ascetic joylessness. I can't say he's my ideal choice for a staff member but these days we're not exactly awash in options. Not awash in students either for that matter," he added wistfully. "With the falling roll the Vice-Chancellor's allocated me one lecturer fewer from next term. As I'm retiring this year I'm hoping he'll hold off until then so my staff can retain their positions."

"If McNally's so ghastly, what makes you think he'll win the Vice-Chancellor over?" Professor Trout asked, puzzled.

"Try arguing with him," the Dean said. "Raise some

current news items until you find one you disagree about, then debate it with him. He'll drive you mad. It's a nightmare: he concedes nothing, absolutely nothing, I tell you; argues every tiny detail in a most offensively tenacious manner; not dishonestly mind you, at least not in his mind. It's all that grim Irish Catholic absolutism in his background. That nonsense is tailored for simpletons to keep them that way, so even though he's now lapsed and intellectually has rejected all that rubbish, the moulding of the man remains." The Dean shuddered at the recollection of McNally's obstinacy.

"Under the circumstances I think I'll take your word for it," Professor Trout said as he topped up the Dean's glass.

The following afternoon McNally came to Professor Trout's office. He curtly declined the Professor's offer of sherry, and also of coffee or tea.

"I do not indulge in stimulants," he said tersely, gazing at the Professor with his piercing dark eyes and emanating an air of wound-up, potentially explosive intensity.

Professor Trout recounted all that had occurred at the meeting with the Vice-Chancellor. "It's a burden I hesitate to impose on you," he said. "However, the Dean has great faith in your capabilities. I'm not sure what new arguments you can put forward, but if you feel you can and are prepared to have a go then I'll organize a meeting with the Vice-Chancellor."

"Do so," McNally snapped. "Let me know when and where," and he rose and left without another word.

When the Vice-Chancellor took Professor Trout's telephone call to arrange the McNally meeting his lifetime's adversarial experiences immediately set his antennae twitching. He instantly agreed with the Professor that perhaps the concerns would be better resolved dealing with a single delegate, while simultaneously his intuition issued a severe storm warning and he buzzed his secretary to bring in McNally's file. His old faithful 'know thine enemy' strategy came into play, suspicion telling him that something ominous was afoot, and he intended to be well prepared.

CHAPTER NINE

APPROXIMATELY EVERY TWO decades two exceptional heavyweights emerge undefeated from the pack to eventually clash, and despite all the pre-fight punditry the result is always impossible to predict. Sometimes the outcome is an unexpectedly quick knock-out; other times a punishing drawn-out bloodbath occurs – as indeed eventuated when the two undefeated-in-debate protagonists, the Vice-Chancellor and McNally, finally locked horns.

Within minutes of the opening bell it dawned on the Vice-Chancellor that here indeed was a rare adversary the like of which he had never encountered, as his opening charm offensive was adroitly side-stepped.

The Vice-Chancellor fell back on the ropes with his tried and true tactic of allowing his foe to punch himself out, but the Irishman was alert to the ploy and cleverly switched the onus back to his opponent. "It is you who are insisting on changes," he said coldly. "Explain why."

"Not changes, Mr McNamara, not changes: reforms," the Vice-Chancellor responded silkily.

"If you suffer from amnesia then by all means call me McNamara," McNally snapped. "If not then it's McNally. Now stop ducking and dodging. Explain why."

"There's an important and positive difference between change and reform," the Vice-Chancellor blustered, alarmed at losing control of the agenda.

"I have no interest in such differences, only the reasons. Explain why."

The Vice-Chancellor endeavoured to do so only to find that every argument, every devious ploy, every cunning word-play which had served him so well for more than two decades was blocked or countered with devastating arguments for which he had neither familiarity nor answer. Unlike any previous opponent the Irishman had not come merely to do battle but with an all-too-apparent determination to triumph.

McNally's attacks were unpredictable in their unorthodoxy, and no matter how often the Vice-Chancellor remarshalled, the Irishman had his number. After an hour's losing combat, in panic and for the first time in his long adversarial career, the Vice-Chancellor decided to settle for a draw and began a dissimulating spoiling strategy by confining his comments to generalities so vague and meaningless as to defy any possibility of contradiction. It was an aptitude he had honed during his merchant banking career when justifying outrageous and unnecessary retainer fees to gullible provincial clients.

"You will I'm sure appreciate, Mr McNally, that in this day and age, taking everything into the fullest consideration and burdensome though it so frequently is, but nevertheless, in the overall scheme of things, university administrators are obliged to weigh a wide range of diverse and often conflicting contingencies in their broad multitude of responsibilities going forward …"

"What is this 'going forward' rubbish?" McNally barked. "That must be the tenth time you've said it. Are you implying there are going backwards, sideways, upwards or downwards options?"

Badly rattled, the Vice-Chancellor, now in full defence mode, stumbled on, the Irishman verbally smacking him from pillar to post in a now largely unanswered assault.

After a further twenty minutes on the receiving end the Vice-Chancellor in desperation fell back on his ultimate defence. "I'm most sympathetic to all that you've said, Mr McNally, but you must understand, at the end of the day I'm only following orders. These reforms are policy decisions by the University Council and I am but a mere servant charged with executing them."

"Absolute garbage!" McNally roared. "I've studied the University Charter. Policy decisions are solely your responsibility to formulate and place before the Council to sanction. These disgraceful occurrences are entirely your personal doing."

Like a battered and bleeding old fighter on the floor, the Vice-Chancellor took an eight count to clear his head. It was the moment of reckoning which ultimately befalls every ageing undefeated champion: the cruel realization that before him now paced a stronger young challenger and his reign was up. But not quite. For it is also the reality of such situations that if outgunned on every front, a single advantage by definition still remains: namely the never-to-be-underestimated value of experience; and long experience now told the befuddled Vice-Chancellor the time had come to abandon the Queensbury rules. Lacking any morality or conscience to act as a restraining referee, the Vice-Chancellor hit McNally with a blow so low and hard as to render him permanently defeated.

"I have been greatly impressed by all that you have said, Mr McNally," he began. "There is no doubt you have given me much to consider and …"

"Reconsider," McNally snarled.

"Yes indeed, reconsider; and you may be assured I shall most certainly do so. The fact that you have given up your valuable time to outline your views is fortuitous, as it was my intention to seek a meeting with you this week anyway."

For the first time the Irishman looked hesitant, a change happily noted by the Vice-Chancellor, who pressed home his attack. "You are doubtless aware that under the new staffing regime, from next term the classics department is to be reduced by one staff member and regrettably, you as the most recently employed will be obliged to forfeit your position."

The Vice-Chancellor watched delighted as alarm spread across McNally's countenance. "Fortunately," he continued, "we do have a single vacancy and I am pleased to inform you that if not quite the field of scholarship to which you are accustomed, nevertheless I have been sufficiently impressed by your advocacy today to put aside any doubts I might otherwise have had as to your capacity to adjust … going forward, Mr McCauley," he added with particular relish.

A month later, now in his new position as the Drama Department's lecturer in stage design, McNally was distressingly spending his days in a room filled with shrieking sodomites. He was a broken man and in the months ahead was often seen wandering about the university muttering incoherently. With all resistance now destroyed the Vice-Chancellor continued uninhibited with his modernization programme.

CHAPTER TEN

WITH THE REBELS' main strike weapon vanquished, and determined to crush any further resistance to his modernization programme, the Vice-Chancellor set about corralling the remaining reactionary forces.

Seemingly overnight, the university's long-admired tree-lined cricket ground was transformed to resemble a Second World War German POW camp after an army of construction workers had rapidly erected 60,000 square feet of wooden-floored, window-lined and skylighted, identical prefabricated barrack-type buildings to house the Humanities faculty's traditional departments.

The Mediaeval Philosophy Department was allocated Shed H, which was subdivided into a receptionless room for the Professor and an adjacent larger room containing a single desk with 30 folding chairs to serve as a lecture theatre. The remaining half of the shed was left empty.

Once again the Professor engaged the Vice-Chancellor; only this time, with the unspoken shift in the balance of power now apparent, he did so by appointment.

"I wish to discuss the temporary premises," he began.

"Temporary; temporary? We have no temporary premises, Professor. There must be some mistake."

"The new barracks you've shifted some of the humanities departments to," Professor Trout elaborated, conscious that the Vice-Chancellor already had him on the back foot.

"Well, dear me, Professor. Hardly temporary and most certainly not barracks. A little patience may be required but I invite you to imagine going forward a mere few years when the new buildings are all linked by attractive pavements and with flower beds alongside the paths and the trees …" Wound up by his own eloquence, the Vice-Chancellor rolled his eyes ceilingward. "Yes, the trees, Professor Minnow, the trees. Imagine. Why, the buildings will be scarcely visible under all the glorious foliage. It will be a veritable Garden of Eden. It's the future, Professor. And the light; have you considered the beneficial effect of all that splendid natural light? No more gloomy rooms in antiquated stone buildings. I must say, I'm surprised. I'd have thought you'd be delighted."

"Well I'm not delighted and nor is anyone else. Furthermore there's no shelving in my study," the Professor complained.

"Shelving? I don't understand."

"Bookshelves, damn it! There are no bookshelves for my books."

"Ah! Now I understand. Bookshelves! Well, you see,

Professor, bookshelves are surprisingly expensive. The Council felt this an opportune moment to introduce the future they aspire to, namely the bookless university."

"I won't have it!" Professor Trout shouted. "This is outrageous. I must have my books."

"Come now, Professor Scallop. Let us look at this logically. Surely you're not inviting me to believe you intend reading, or perhaps I should say in some cases rereading, all of your books. And even if you do so intend, well, the regrettable fact is that you could not and nor could your students. I suppose it is theoretically possible should some hypothetical student aged 20 with the financial wherewithal to devote every waking hour for the rest of his or her life solely to the task of reading your books, and assuming that person lived to a ripe old age, then he or she might actually fulfil that ambition. But that, I respectfully suggest, is scarcely your situation, Professor, and I venture, no matter how admirably studious your pupils may be, it is not the ambition of any of them, or indeed any other living soul.

"So you see, when viewed that way it is not only quite illogical for the university to indulge in a wasteful shelving expense just to display your library when it is apparent its sole function is ornamental, but on a more positive note, it is as I have alluded to, an excellent opportunity to show to the world the new bookless university we aspire to going forward."

The Professor's mind raced. It was an intolerable state of affairs but he was now devoid of resistance. He recalled his student days nearly five decades earlier and the shared untidy flats with their makeshift bookcases of wooden planks supported by bricks. It would be unbecoming, but if necessary he would do it. Then again, he pondered, perhaps he could retain a hundred or so volumes and the remainder could go in the rehoused departmental library in a specially separated section. Considering this reminded him of a fresh problem.

"Another matter," he said tersely. "The space you've left empty for rehousing the mediaeval philosophy library is quite unsuitable. Despite the blinds I noticed were in place there's still too much light. Most of those books are centuries old and of incalculable value. Important security issues arise. Covering the windows with blinds will be superfluous as the walls will be needed for the books. And then there's temperature control and also the fire risk which …"

"I'm afraid you're quite mistaken Professor," the Vice-Chancellor interrupted. "We have no intention of using that space for such a purpose." He stopped and rustled among some papers on his desk. "Ah! Here we are. Now let me see. Yes … mediaeval philosophy … Shed H. Ah yes." He looked up. "That currently vacant space is intended for one of our proposed new disciplines opening in a fortnight. The Council believes very strongly in the importance of mixing the old and the new. Each will assist the other: the one to aid in introducing the university's traditions worthy of retention; the other to facilitate a more modern outlook going forward among the established disciplines. I have no doubt it will be a mutually enriching experience."

Professor Trout felt faint. "And who or what will be sharing my barracks?"

"Not barracks, Professor; not barracks. Once the trees are in full bloom you will ..."

"Who am I sharing the premises with?"

"Of course; let me see." The Vice-Chancellor re-examined his papers. "Ah yes: a most exciting new discipline; indeed a world first. All of our research suggests a very considerable untapped market. Our new School of Paedophiliac Studies will be housed there. Apparently their studies will be confined to film shows rather than old-fashioned lectures, which explains why blinds are required. We will be looking to you and your staff to make the newcomers welcome and assist with introducing them to academic life. Naturally, given the number of paedophiles the authorities claim exist, it's probable the new department will quickly outgrow the space allocated and require its own building. It was suggested to me that we approach the Vatican to fund the Chair. I'm told they have a particular interest in this subject. Once in their own premises I envisage there will be numerous organizations receptive to the naming rights sponsorship opportunity. I'm also told Baden-Powell House has been mooted as having just the right ring about it."

"School of Paedophiliac Studies?" the Professor exploded. "This is scandalous."

"Not at all, Professor Tadpole. You simply haven't come to terms with contemporary thinking in higher education. I'm afraid you persist in retaining the unhealthy and now properly redundant, and I might add, in many modern educationalists' minds, the somewhat patronizing belief that higher education should be elitist and confined to a handful of esoteric subjects clearly beyond the comprehension of most citizens. It is an undemocratic and put plainly, if you will forgive me, a selfish attitude, now rightfully discarded. One has only to examine the booming new line-dancing department to appreciate the virtues of the new order. Our psychology department subjected the line-dancing scholars to IQ tests and discovered all fell into the moronic category, indeed in some cases even lower. Yet those line-dancing scholars will leave this institution dignified by the possession of university degrees, something hitherto inconceivable. It makes me very proud, Professor Marlin, to be in the vanguard of outside-the-square, progressive education. You must understand that the new higher education thinking going forward is that every human endeavour is worthy of advanced study."

"Paedophilia – a human endeavour?"

"Perhaps you misunderstand, Professor. The new school will be studying paedophilia. No practical classes are intended."

Professor Trout's mind was awhirl. Through the confusion he suddenly recalled the mediaeval philosophy library issue. If this disgraceful new activity was going into the adjacent area then where was the library to go, he asked.

"Splendidly rehoused. A strikingly elegant building is to be constructed for it. We have firm undertakings on that point."

"I trust it will be appropriately close to our new premises," Professor Trout said.

"No," the Vice-Chancellor replied dreamily. "I'm afraid it

will be some distance away. In the United States, to be precise. Princeton University outbid everyone. For a time it appeared Harvard would prevail, but such was the fervour shown by ten rival American universities that Sotheby's estimate of £1.5 million was soon passed and in the event Princeton paid £2.2 million. Of course it's wonderful news for Ralston – and in a wider sense, for British higher education. It is the proceeds from that sale which have enabled us to construct the fine new Humanities faculty buildings and, additionally, start our new schools of higher learning such as line-dancing and paedo-philiac studies. On the other hand, speaking altruistically, one does feel a slight concern that some American universities should remain so entrenched in the old values. I am not a historian, Professor Sprat, but I believe it is the sort of backward thinking that has marked the fall of every great power. Frankly, I see the sale as symbolic of America's inevitable decline. The question I ask myself is should we …"

Professor Trout could endure no more, and without a word he rose and left.

Back at his study he found Frewen waiting, plainly agitated. "I need your advice," he whined. "Beefy's told me I have to fatten up. Put on a minimum 60 pounds by Christmas if I'm to keep the job. She says I lack empathy with the fat girls and am setting a poor example; she says …"

"She's absolutely right," the Professor snapped. "You're living in the past, Frewen; not a modernist at all. Now leave me alone," and, startled by this untypically curt response, Frewen scurried out.

For ten minutes the Professor sat with his head in his hands. It was the end of the road. He'd had enough. He could manage on his pension – but doing what? Perhaps another book. Writing full-time he could complete a book in a year. He'd often felt there was a serious gap in the absence of an introductory mediaeval philosophy tome: a sort of primer aimed at new students. His spirits rose a little. He'd think about it, discuss it that evening with Enid, indeed; and he turned to the unopened mail on his desk.

Three philosophy journals; a notice of a forthcoming philosophy conference in Milan and another for a summer seminar in Colorado; an enquiry from a literary magazine as to whether they could send a new philosophy book for review – "sadly our budget only allows a £150 fee for 3000 words" the letter added; an unintelligible and anonymous lunatic's letter of abuse with a Cork postmark – philosophy academics, Professor Trout knew from long experience, were popular targets for such missives – and last, a letter from Walter King.

Splendid here; far better than I expected. Very lively and stimulating academic scene. Unlike Ralston, lots of talking shop. Scotland's oldest university mind you so perhaps not surprising. We have our share of nonsense courses but they're very much in the background. No problem with language either. The natives actually speak English. Apparently the unintelligible Scot brogue is only a problem in the west and far north.

You probably won't be interested but are you

aware your counterpart here, Professor Rankin, had the misfortune to suffer a fairly severe heart attack last week? He's calling it quits at the end of the term and they're now left high and dry in their mediaeval philosophy department. Personally I think you should consider a step-in appointment as Professor for a few years. You know what they say about the stimulatory virtues of a change and I can tell you from my own experience, it's been highly invigorating.

Think about it and let me know soon. I took the liberty of telling the Humanities Dean I would put the idea to you and he said they'd be delighted to have you.

Now a favour please. Would you consider allowing us to publish your book? I can put it in the forthcoming list if you give me the go-ahead now. Call me.

Best wishes,

Walter

PS: It won't surprise you to learn that I've taken up golf. I play twice weekly with two classics lecturers.

On reading this, Professor Trout's elation at the publication offer was also tinged with a pang of envy. Enid had often urged him to take up golf but for most of the last decade his weekends had been occupied in writing his book.

He scanned the letterhead. There was an email and fax address. Quickly he drafted a hand-written note.

Dear Walter,

The Huns have finally penetrated the walls here. All is lost. You escaped just in time. Please proceed with the book. I'll discuss coming up with Enid. Personally it has great appeal but naturally I must consider her feelings and then there's the house to think about and other issues. I will telephone tomorrow, at 11am.

PS: If I come perhaps I'll join you with the golf. Am I too old to learn?

After three false starts he succeeded in faxing it, then, gathering his satchel and happier than he had been in memory, he went home early.

CHAPTER ELEVEN

"DOUBLE-WHAMMY CELEBRITY VISITORS: EDUC-
ATION MINISTER AND DAVIAN THIRST COMING
TO RALSTON," the latest issue of the university newspaper
headlined across its front page.

Perplexed, Professor Trout read the accompanying article
with a growing sense of alienation from the contemporary
world. The story read:

> The Vice-Chancellor announced on Tuesday that next
> month the high-profile Education Minister will visit
> Ralston, a university the Minister described in the
> Commons last week as "epitomizing all best practice
> in progressive tertiary education reform".
>
> The Minister will address a luncheon, to be
> attended by all Ralston professors, on the topic "The
> Alignment of Contemporary Values with Government
> Higher Education Policy."

The Minister's meteoric political rise is generally attributed to his avant-garde outlook and reforming zeal. It is no surprise that he currently registers top position in the Preferred Prime Minister polls with the 18-25 age bracket. The Minister is frequently in the news. Last month he released an album of his education reform speeches, rendered by him personally in rap music format and recorded at Brixton Prison to background drumming provided by Rastafarian inmates.

Earlier this year, only a week after his highly publicised marriage to the stunning Sudanese model, Shania, he admitted to having a tattoo bearing the message "Pay As You Enter" across his buttocks, which he stated was intended as a gesture of solidarity with the gay community and consistent with his personal political agenda of representing only the real people. The Minister was single-handedly responsible for the substitution in secondary schools of Gay Studies for history, and his current campaign against teaching mathematics has attracted much support from students across the land.

Equally exciting is the news that the Minister will be accompanied by the internationally acclaimed installation sculptor, Davian Thirst, who is known to be a close friend. Mr Thirst has agreed to judge the inaugural Smatchi-Ralston Installation Art Festival, following which the Minister will present the winner's prize.

Ralston's Academy of Installation Art, although less than two years old, now boasts over 80 pupils.

The festival will be an annual event intended to place Ralston in the forefront of the post-post-modernist school of contemporary art.

The famous publicist and wealthy installation art collector Gerald Smatchi has endowed a £100,000 fund to provide the prizes each year and is also expected to attend.

Earlier this year Mr Smatchi generously offered his personal Thirst collection to the nation, subject to the government providing suitable permanent premises. The Minister of Culture recently announced that negotiations were progressing satisfactorily with the Church of England commissioners, to take over Lambeth Palace to house the collection. It is intended the Palace will be renamed the Thirst Museum.

Over the following weeks the installation art contest became the cause of considerable consternation. When one exhibit, spread across the quad, comprising ten faeces-smeared babies' potties interspersed with a series of broken toys and a doll with a carving knife through its head, was gathered up and dumped by the elderly head porter, Geoffrey Cone, the Vice-Chancellor promptly issued a notice which was plastered throughout the university.

NOTICE

The forthcoming Smatchi-Ralston Festival of Installation Art is the most important and momentous event in the university's history.

Over the next few weeks the various entries will be assembled throughout the campus. Following an unfortunate incident arising through carelessness, one important exhibit has already been inadvertently destroyed.

Going forward, students and staff are urged to take the utmost care to ensure no repetition of this deeply regrettable occurrence.

Vice-Chancellor

As the exhibits began to appear around the university, confusion arose. Rubbish bins overflowed as the cleaners, who had been singled out for a special warning lecture by the Vice-Chancellor, adopted an ultra-cautionary approach and concentrated on dusting, unsure as to what were exhibits and what was rubbish.

A comatose Rubenesque Studies fat girl lay unattended in a hallway for six hours after collapsing with a heart attack and attracted considerable praise as a likely winning exhibit.

Professor Rohan Hill entered his office one day to find all of his windows painted black except for one which was smashed. A bulldozer axle extended through it, one end resting on his desk. This exhibit, entitled Transcendent Metamorphosis, symbolised the industrial age's conflicts, according to the descriptive placard beside it.

Professor Trout did not remain untouched by all of this. On arrival one morning he found the path to his barracks door blocked by an old dentist chair on which sat, propped up, a decapitated sheep with a notice hanging round the stump of its neck bearing the words "I AM" in large block letters.

His senior lecturer, Margaret Clark, greeted him. "I've already been on to the Vice-Chancellor, Professor, but I'm afraid my complaint fell on deaf ears."

"Why does it have to go here?" Professor Trout demanded angrily.

"I raised that and suggested it be shifted. The Vice-Chancellor said he would make enquiries. He called me back a few minutes later and insisted it has to stay here as the artist claims the location is an integral part of the creation. Apparently it's symbolic of a cultural clash and is entitled Mediaeval Angst. Being positioned adjacent to our doorway, according to its creator, is fundamental to its essence, whatever that's supposed to mean."

"I won't have it!" Professor Trout exploded and he stormed off to the Vice-Chancellor's office. Ducking beneath a cord stretched across the administration building's entrance from which hung sixty stretched condoms interspersed with dangling swastikas, this another exhibit entitled Response to Dachau, he entered the Vice-Chancellor's office. But he was soon on the back foot as the Vice-Chancellor launched into him.

"I will not tolerate this lack of co-operation Professor

Roe. The forthcoming installation art festival is of immense importance to this university and the obstructive attitude, conspicuously from the older humanities disciplines," he emphasized darkly, "simply reinforces the anachronistic nature of your activities."

Professor Trout valiantly endeavoured to fight back but the Vice-Chancellor quickly interrupted and held up his hands. "No, I will not hear another word. It's a simple matter for you to step round the exhibit for the remaining ten days until the judging. Goodness me, Professor Dolphin, you're scarcely inconvenienced compared with other departments, most of whom, I might add, are entering into the spirit of the festival and share this university's justifiable pride in the installation art pupils' accomplishments.

"Look at the grief-counselling department. Not a squeak from them, yet they've been obliged to suspend all grief counselling workshops following the installation of one of the exhibits. I freely confess I don't entirely comprehend all of these entries – in the grief-counselling case apparently a musical farm tractor playing the same Doris Day song over and over again. There seems to be a common theme revolving round cultural clash topics with most of the entries. I profess no artistic disposition but rather feel this topic is lacking somewhat in imagination. Therein lies the beauty of open competition, as doubtless the winner will stand above the common herd. We shall see; we shall see. Nevertheless I will not stand in the path of progress and creative endeavour and I ask no more of you than the same."

When Professor Trout again began to protest the Vice-Chancellor immediately stopped him. "Not a word, not a word. I have enough problems as it is with the installation art department. Unfortunately the Professor of Installation Art has not been taking his pills lately and there have been some rather unfortunate occurrences. Your and the other old-fashioned humanities disciplines' constant complaining has wasted a great deal of my time and induced me to hasten the reform agenda. On Friday I will be addressing a meeting of the entire humanities staff and will outline the forthcoming humanities departments reforms going forward. Now, if you please, Professor Skate, I have work to do," and he picked up his pen and began to write.

Despondent, Professor Trout trudged back to his barracks.

CHAPTER TWELVE

THE RUMBLE OF grumbling voices abruptly ceased and a detectable tremor rippled through the auditorium when the Vice-Chancellor suddenly appeared from a side-door and strode briskly to the podium. Above him were suspended two car tyres, a refrigerator door, some grubby-looking underwear and a set of bagpipes, this incongruous cluster – entitled Cultural Dichotomy – comprising another installation arts festival entry. The Vice-Chancellor beamed down at the assembled 226 humanities teaching staff.

"Good afternoon colleagues, and thank you for allowing me some of your valuable time," he began. "I do not intend to keep you very long, however, in recent weeks some of you have been gracious enough to express to me your uncertainty arising from this university's progressive changes intended going forward. In the circumstances I felt it appropriate to call this meeting and explain the University Council's policies, so as to avoid any further confusion."

"Bloody Vietcong re-education programme," a Latin lecturer sitting next to Professor Trout muttered.

"I shall begin with some hard facts," the Vice-Chancellor continued. "The first goes without saying, namely that as an institution we cannot survive unless revenue exceeds income. The current restructuring programme will ensure we remain on a permanently sound financial footing, to everyone's benefit. Furthermore, that is a necessary prerequisite to achieving the government's medium-term objective of privatizing Ralston. Once we have a Stock Exchange listing and so long as we maintain profitability, future expansion can be funded by conventional capital-raising on the Exchange."

This announcement was greeted with guarded suspicion, the Stock Exchange and its mysteries being beyond the interest of most of the audience although they recognized the word "privatization" as one of the "bad" things of Thatcherism.

The Vice-Chancellor, drawing on his past trade-unionist experiences, had anticipated an uproar at the mention of privatization and, pleasantly surprised at its absence, he continued more boldly.

"You will be aware that over the past four decades, participation in university education in Britain has risen from 5% to 35% of all school pupils. That is an impressive growth achievement. The University Council wholeheartedly supports the government's ambition to ultimately ensure every citizen receives a university degree, and we intend making such adjustments to our current curricula as are necessary to facilitate that objective. Those innovations also accord with our intention to maintain a sound financial foundation.

"As you know, the university is funded from a number of sources but principally the central government grant, student fees and some commercial sponsorship of departmental chairs. In respect of the latter, and mindful that central government funding per pupil has halved over the past two decades, we intend becoming pro-active going forward, in marketing naming rights for both Chairs and the many fine new buildings the Humanities faculty now enjoys."

An angry murmuring broke out at mention of the barracks. Ignoring this, the Vice-Chancellor plunged on. "We shall also learn from our American colleagues, whose universities are substantially funded by alumni endowments whereas in Britain less than 3% of university finance stems from such sources. There is, however, one particular monetary source the University Council has decided to target and that is the fee-paying foreign student. Why, you ask? Because foreign students are obliged to pay a substantial premium for access to our educational facilities to offset the taxpayer contribution. Such revenue increments will allow us greater scope for expansion of our many fine new disciplines, to everyone's benefit."

Another outbreak of grumbling followed reference to the new disciplines but again the Vice-Chancellor continued unperturbed.

"Accordingly, Ralston intends becoming the foremost foreign-student university in the United Kingdom and to that end I have pleasure in announcing the commencement of a new, fully funded scholarship programme with a single objective. Resulting from this initiative, Ralston will be able to boast of being the world's only university with students from all 200-plus nations on earth. We believe the status arising from this will in itself make Ralston a preferred university choice for students in the new competitive environment going forward.

"The scholarships will be for two pupils from remote nations such as Mongolia, Bolivia, the Congo and countries not already represented here on their citizens' own initiative. These new foreign students will require a special tolerance on your part in acknowledging their varying tastes, language difficulties and practices. We have already taken the necessary action with the education authorities in such countries and the new students will all be with us within a month. They will be provided with dormitory accommodation similar to and adjacent the handsome new structures the Humanities faculty now enjoys."

Further derisory snorts rang around the auditorium.

"There is one other reform we intend. Henceforth three-year bachelor degrees in the traditional humanities subjects which are retained, are to be condensed to two years. Obviously, as evident by student numbers, the provenly successful exciting new humanities departments such as Rubenesque Studies and Grief Counselling will continue with three-year degrees. We believe this progressive action will be an attractive spur in arresting the declining humanities rolls and also provide us with a competitive advantage over rival universities placing more demanding obligations on their pupils."

Gasps of disbelief echoed across the auditorium but ceased as the Vice-Chancellor continued.

"Some humanities pursuits will necessarily be terminated to make room for our more popular new fields of study. That is a sensible move, not only for Ralston but because those closed departments' few potential students will strengthen the numbers in other less progressive universities still offering such courses, and in the process achieve a much-needed economy of scale."

"Destroy the people to save them," the Latin lecturer muttered angrily.

"The closure of traditional courses deemed obsolete will be a continuing programme. Over the next few years Ralston will gradually reposition itself through a strategy of introducing popular new scholarship subjects so as to eventually be confined to, and possess, an effective monopoly on those disciplines by dint of its leader-in-the-field, pioneering role, a state of affairs any sensible businessman will tell you is highly desirable."

A palpable shiver of fear now passed through the room, detected through long experience by the Vice-Chancellor who happily sensed he had his audience on the back foot. He continued, "We will allow our rival universities to compete among themselves in the conventional anachronistic pursuits. We, however, shall not be so foolish. If there is any doubt about the wisdom of that approach then again I would draw your attention to the new fields of scholarship Ralston has already pioneered, such as our admirable departments of Astrology or Rubenesque Studies, both of which are enjoying massive student growth."

This was too much, and emboldened by a sense of collective security and therefore anonymity, an uproar of dissenting voices erupted. Cries of "Barbarism!", "Vandalism!", "Sacrilege!" and even cat-calls rent the air. The Vice-Chancellor waited patiently, content in the knowledge that he held all the cards, a fleeting smile crossing his features. It was an all-too-familiar scene from his former company receivership career. Eventually he raised his hands for silence.

"I am pleased my announcement has stimulated your interest," he said. "Understandably many of you are concerned about your own positions. Please put your minds at rest. The new, modern Ralston University will require a considerably larger teaching staff than at present, and while a small adjustment in your personal spheres of tuition expertise will be required, I have no doubt about your ability to cope." He paused. "There is one other announcement I have pleasure in making. From today, consistent with our modernization policy, the university's motto is to be changed."

This information was received with stunned silence, the academics now fully aware of their impotence.

"The current motto Optima Durant or 'Quality Endures' has been rightly deemed by the Council to be outmoded on two counts. First, it has the unsavoury ring of elitism. Under the new democratic order going forward we intend that everyone will endure, and not just the intellectually advantaged. In any event the Council rejects the word 'endure', carrying as it does the negative and discouraging inference of difficulty and sending quite the wrong message to potential Ralston scholars. We wish our students to approach higher education without fear of failure, and we intend ensuring that in future all of our pupils complete their degrees effortlessly and free of pressure. Such an objective is consistent with the march of civilization in eliminating difficulty from our everyday lives, and we see no reason why young people should be an exception and subject to onerous and unnecessary intellectual rigour.

"Finally, and arguably most disturbing, the current postulate is expressed in Latin, a dead language symbolising the past, which is most certainly not the image Ralston seeks. The university's new motto will be easily understood for it is in plain English and therefore welcoming for all. It is Degrees for Everyone. The change will take effect once our consultants have completed their investigations into our intended new coat of arms. I have taken up much of your valuable time and I thank you," and abruptly the Vice-Chancellor turned and strode quickly off the stage – fortuitously timed as it transpired, for seconds later one of the tyres crashed to where he had been standing, rolled across the stage and flattened an elderly poetry lecturer.

Professor Trout looked at his neighbour. Rendered speechless, the Latin lecturer, now ashen faced, was gazing vacantly at the empty stage. Amid the hubbub of angry voices the Professor rose and left.

Back in his study he found among his mail a letter from Theopopolus. It was on a Princeton University letterhead with the imprint at the top, "Dr Eugene Theopopolus, M.A.

(Harvard) Ph.D. (Ralston), Lecturer, Mediaeval Philosophy Department".

Dear Professor Trout,

As you can see I have secured a mediaeval philosophy lecturership at Princeton. They read my thesis and that, combined with the prestige of a Ralston doctorate, carried the day in the face of some fairly stiff competition. Mediaeval philosophy and its associated fields are popular here so I feel rather pleased with myself. Also, the University Press is publishing my thesis in book form shortly – hard cover too, so I'll send a copy if you don't mind it gracing your shelves. I suppose you'll think they're insane for publishing it. Perhaps we have less demanding standards here in America.

My purpose in writing is twofold.

First, a month ago my Professor called me in and said your library was for sale. Naturally I was astonished as I couldn't imagine you ever letting it go but he showed me the tender documents so presumably you had your reasons. As I had been at Ralston he put me in charge of purchasing it. There was fierce bidding from rival universities but we prevailed by paying the full breakup value as I suspect some of our rivals were intending to dispose of some of the special treasures, which would be a tragedy.

My professor raised the funds inside three days. He telephoned around the alumni in the financial industries: sharebrokers, bankers and those types, and arranged a trade-off. In return for a month's head-start with their annual roadshows to our department's graduates for management trainee positions, they quickly came up with the funds, including another two million dollars to construct a building to house the library, so you can rest assured it will remain intact and in good hands. The new building design is magnificent and has state-of-the-art air-temperature controls which will ensure the library's survival. Everyone is very thrilled at securing it.

The other matter I wish to raise is to thank you for my years at Ralston. I found your post-graduate classes and tutorials wonderfully stimulating and will remain forever grateful. I'll do my best to emulate you but that won't be easy, not least because of the sheer number of students. As I said, philosophy and similar disciplines are immensely popular here so we can't achieve the enviable intimacy of the Ralston environment. Our commercial world seems to place a premium on our graduates, which may explain the high student numbers.

Again, my heart-felt thanks.

Eugene Theopopolus

Professor Trout finished reading the letter with mixed emotions, his previous dismay at the loss of his beloved library now partly tempered by Theopopolus's assurances. He felt like a Nazi death-camp victim heading to the gas chamber, who had just been told his child was safely in America. Now all that remained was a sense of impending doom.

CHAPTER THIRTEEN

BUZZ OF EXCITEMENT was evident throughout the university on the day of the visit by the Education Minister and Davian Thirst, the presence of celebrities being something to which Ralston was unaccustomed.

A nervously whispered attempt by some traditional humanities professors to organise a boycott of the luncheon soon petered out, not only through fear of the Vice-Chancellor's wrath, although that was sufficient to terminate any rebellion, but more through a lack of support. The humanities professors' curiosity to see and hear the famous visitors matched that of the students and overwhelmed any mutinous sentiments they might possess. Even Professor Trout felt celebratory, for today would hopefully see the removal of the installation art exhibit outside his door. There had been a heavy downpour four days earlier following which Mediaeval Angst had rapidly deteriorated and was now fly-blown and odoriferous.

Thirst, wearing dark glasses, descended from a helicopter at 11am, holding aloft two helium-filled balloons, one shaped as a gorilla and the other as a child's doll. After being gushingly greeted by the Vice-Chancellor and a doting entourage of administrative staff, he insisted on inspecting and judging the installation art exhibits, unaccompanied and at his own pace.

At midday the 108 invited senior academics assembled in the Great Hall for the luncheon, the traditional humanities professors all placed at the rear. At the head table the beaming Vice-Chancellor sat centre-place. On his right was the Education Minister, pony-tailed and pin-striped and wearing a black silk skivvy in lieu of a shirt and tie, and a gold ring in his right earlobe.

To the Vice-Chancellor's left sat Davian Thirst, still wearing his dark glasses, the balloons now tied to his chair and floating above him. His hair was dyed green and he was bare-chested beneath a shimmering orange plastic suit. Resting on his chest was a freshly severed chicken's head at the end of a gold chain.

Also at the head table, but conventionally attired, were Gerald Smatchi, the new Chancellor Robert Gwyther and the stolid Mayor of Ralston, his chains of office draped across his front, while at the table's end, barefooted and jabbering incoherently to himself while periodically rocking with jolting spasms of private mirth, was the denim-clad Professor of Installation Art, who had plainly again failed to take his pills.

Professor Trout endeavoured to engage his neighbours in

conversation – in vain, as it transpired, for the Vice-Chancellor had personally attended to the seating arrangements as part of his ongoing harassment campaign against the traditional humanities. Thus the Professor's dining companions were respectively the business administration and line-dancing professors – the former, Professor Trout wrongly assuming, rendered speechless by the glittering occasion although in fact he was too relentlessly dreary to make conversation under any circumstances; the latter barely articulate and engrossed in methodically working his way single-handedly through two bottles of wine.

When the luncheon was concluded, and after coffee had been served and port passed around, the Vice-Chancellor rose and addressed the assembled diners.

"This is a proud and historic day for Ralston University," he began. "Not only is it the first-ever visit by an Education Minister to this institution, but what gives it special import, and I say this without fear of contradiction" – an unnecessary injunction given that the Vice-Chancellor and the professors all knew he could as well say "one and one are three" without fear of contradiction – "is that we are graced by the presence of a Titan who I have no doubt history will record as the greatest reforming Education Minister in our history."

Despite the disappointing absence of applause the Minister affected a grave demeanour and with a small nod, acknowledged the Vice-Chancellor's accolade.

"We are also overwhelmingly honoured," the Vice-Chancellor continued, "by the presence of one of the truly extraordinary figures in British art history, the world-renowned Davian Thirst, who has generously given up his time to be with us today and has already this morning inspected the many magnificent installation art entries. Mr Thirst will announce the winner following the Minister's address. I invite you all to then join the head table and inspect the first Smatchi-Ralston Installation Art Festival winning entry. Without further ado I now call upon the Minister to address us," whereupon the Vice-Chancellor began loudly clapping and, to the Minister's relief, the assembly duly followed.

At this juncture, without explanation, a wheelchaired black dwarf emerged from backstage and rolled across to a position adjacent to the Professor of Installation Art. As the Minister commenced speaking the midget began flamboyantly gesticulating with his hands, accompanied by gruesome facial grimacing for emphasis. This figure was the Minister's latest fashion initiative – a sign-language exponent with the additional attributes of being a dwarf, paraplegic and black.

After the usual pleasantries the Education Minister warmed to his task. Ralston, he said, was in the vanguard of the new thinking and was a standard-bearer for the government's tertiary education reforms. There were certain key principles the government felt strongly about, epitomized by Ralston's enterprise. Education for its own sake he personally considered a bit dodgy, and the idea that you could learn about the world by reading books was self-evidently wrong. A relationship with the workplace was what was important.

Ralston University, the Minister asserted, was at the cutting edge of the twenty-first-century approach to higher education. The Vice-Chancellor was a revolutionary visionary and, the Minister hinted, would soon be appropriately recognized by the Queen for his achievements.

At this point the Minister's address was interrupted by a piercing scream from the Professor of Installation Art, who rose on uncertain legs and launched a diving attack on the dwarf, spilling him from his wheelchair. When this embarrassment had been tidied up, the Professor having been escorted gibbering off the stage and the dwarf restored to his wheelchair, the Minister resumed.

The Vice-Chancellor's admirably ambitious plans to franchise the Ralston University brand throughout Eastern Europe, sub-Saharan Africa and India, the Minister said, aside from making a significant contribution to Britain's invisible trade earnings, would additionally assist those underdeveloped regions to acquire the very best of western civilization's values.

Periodically, led by the Vice-Chancellor, the address was interspersed with applause, and encouraged by this, the Minister raised his voice to signify the importance of his finishing remarks.

"The time has come," he said sternly, "to abandon the classics, history, English, philosophy and the other utterly redundant traditional university courses and to embrace the modern world and substitute reality.

"On behalf of the government I give you a pledge. Henceforth this administration will do all in its power to delete the stain of high-browism from tertiary education. The Oxbridge and Ivy League days belong in the past. Our policy is clear; and that, simply put, is a university education for everyone."

The Vice-Chancellor now leapt flamboyantly to his feet and instigated a final round of applause, remaining standing in an endeavour to sustain it as long as possible. Professor Trout and his traditional humanities colleagues sat stoically in silence.

Next the Vice-Chancellor introduced Davian Thirst. Mr Thirst, he advised, had generously donated one of his own works to Ralston as a beginning to the university's intended installation art collection, whereupon to loud applause Thirst rose and presented the two balloons to the Vice-Chancellor. Smatchi leant forward, eying the balloons hungrily. Two weeks later he would boast of his coup in buying these from the Vice-Chancellor for a bargain £25,000.

To a generous ovation Thirst now seized the microphone, gripping it in both hands like a pop-singer.

"Fanks," he began. "Fing is, see, life's full of sorta basic fings and art's gotta duty t' society to reflect those cultural clashes and that sorta fing. So how's art do that in the post-post-modernist age? I'll tell ya. S'ony one way and that's t' use the symbolic elements of society's dross to demonstrate frew subversion, the spiritual troofs of efryday existence."

He continued in this vein for a few more minutes then said, "Time's come to 'nounce the winner. Gotta tell ya some of the entries 'ave a spiritual dimension which's cut deep into me personal psyche and I bleve should be in our major gallery c'lections. Also gotta tell ya there was one stand-out entry. S'a truly great masterpiece and back in London I intend mentioning it to the Tate. It must be safed for the nation.

"Lays and genamen," he concluded, "the winner is ..." and he paused theatrically, "Untitled!"

Applause broke out, Thirst sat down and the Vice-Chancellor rose again. "I now invite you all to join the head table and accompany us to the winning exhibit, where the Minister has graciously consented to present the prize."

With a clatter of chairs the assembly rose and followed the head-table worthies out into the quad, where waiting were the 87 installation art students, as motley a rabble as had ever graced Ralston. Having been strictly forbidden to attend the campus that morning while Thirst made his evaluations, they now mobbed their hero and for ten minutes chaos reigned. Eventually order was restored.

"Mr Thirst will now lead us to the winning exhibit," the Vice-Chancellor bawled. "Please allow him room," and Thirst, followed by the head-table dignitaries, then the professors and, as strictly instructed by the Vice-Chancellor, the installation art students trailing in the rear, set out in an unruly trek across the quad.

Thirst stopped before the double doors of the ancient centrepiece chapel, threw them open and turned to the waiting audience.

"Lays and genamen, I gif you the winner: Untitled," he bawled.

The crowd pressed forward into the chapel, then with cries of alarm halted; for there before them, hanging from the rafters, dead eyes bulging in his purple, swollen-tongue-lolling face, was McNally, unwittingly the first-ever Smatchi-Ralston Installation Art Prize-winning exhibit, and now finally at peace with the world.

CHAPTER FOURTEEN

"CAN'T SAY I'M SURPRISED," the Dean of Humanities and Professor of Classics said casually to Professor Trout an hour later in the Dean's study where they had retreated to the solace of whisky, a rare treat reflecting the gravity of the occasion.

"Oh? Why's that?" Professor Trout asked, still traumatised after glimpsing the sorry spectacle of McNally's grossly distorted, suspended figure.

"Of course Aristotle would have disapproved," the classics professor continued blithely. "But then again, his opposition to suicide didn't reflect the prevailing view in ancient Greek society."

"You mean it was accepted?" Professor Trout enquired.

"Absolutely; and there's the give-away clue. Don't you see? McNally knew that with the ancient Greeks suicide was more or less considered obligatory if one felt dishonoured in any way. However, there were qualifications. An honourable suicide meant the sword; McNally would have been fully aware the rope was considered ignoble in ancient Greece, and therein lies the explanation."

"I'm afraid you've lost me," Professor Trout said. "If you'll forgive me, I must say you are taking a surprisingly nonchalant view of this tragedy."

"Nonchalant?" the Dean refilled his glass. "Tragedy? Mmm," he mused and then, after a contemplative pause, "I'm afraid I can't forgive McNally. If I'm not mistaken Britain still retains capital punishment for traitors and as far as I'm concerned that sums up McNally's fate in a nutshell. As you sow, etc. … Pity McNally didn't practise that biblical injunction he'd have known so well. No; I'm afraid he got what he deserved."

"Now you've certainly lost me," Professor Trout muttered.

"All perfectly clear to me," the Dean said sharply. "The Vice-Chancellor would have been mincemeat arguing against McNally. I told you at the time. McNally was relentless. Not a man after my own heart, I freely concede, but I blame him for all that's occurred. He agreed to sort the Vice-Chancellor out but what did he do instead when you arranged the showdown? Oiled his way in to sneakily engineer a career change he obviously secretly coveted, and left us all in the lurch. If he'd gone in to bat for us as he promised, he'd have butchered the Vice-Chancellor and we wouldn't be in this intolerable situation. As far as I'm concerned it's utterly unforgivable, and I trust his widow doesn't call on me to speak at his funeral."

Now baffled, Professor Trout sought further clarification.

"Fit the pieces of the jigsaw together and I think you will get the picture," the Dean said smugly, plainly enjoying his Holmesian role.

"Jigsaw? What on earth do you mean?"

"Consider McNally's history. First the seminary – and we all know what that involves," the Dean nodded knowingly.

"You're surely not suggesting he killed himself through guilt at leaving?" Professor Trout asked, bemused.

"Oh no," the Dean chuckled. "Guilt, yes. That goes with the territory, with all that ghastly Irish Catholic relic-worshipping and fearmongering. But not for leaving the seminary. No guilt there. It all makes perfect sense to me and frankly, I'm surprised you can't see it – the bigger picture, that is."

"Well I can't," Professor Trout said sharply.

"Add it all up. He walks from the seminary. Claims he's lost his faith. That, I concede, may have been true but equally it may be irrelevant. Then he marries; no children," the Dean added ominously. "No surprise either, if you saw his wife. One doesn't want – " he hesitated – "I don't wish to be unkind but …" and again he paused, "well … if you saw the wife, and without putting too fine a point on it, it's inconceivable – you know – the business end of marriage … I mean one simply can't imagine, as it were … well I'm sure you get the picture. His marriage was plainly a sham. And another thing. He had a collection of Mario Lanza records and a miniature in his study of Michelangelo's 'David', which just about puts the final seal on the matter. "

Now totally confused, Professor Trout said, "I really have no idea what you're trying to tell me."

"Oh, come now. You read the newspapers. Think about it: he starts with the seminary, which everyone knows is a pervert's paradise, then out he goes, puts up the cover of orthodoxy by marrying – well, he didn't fool me," the Dean added darkly, "then at the first opportunity he sells us all down the river and seizes his opportunity to grease his way into stage design and thespianism, and we certainly know all about that. Prancing poofters, the lot of them. Came home, he obviously did, and from my point of view that was the final straw. Don't misunderstand me. If it was good enough for Socrates to indulge in then far be it from me to criticize. Personally, all of that's McNally's business, but if satisfying his true leanings is what he wanted, well I for one would have respected him if he'd been more open about it. With discretion, mind you. Can't say I share this modern belief that sodomy is some sort of art form. But of course frankness was out of the question. Instead he opted for a private danse macabre; a pas de deux with his baser instincts if you like, and all that entrenched Catholic guilt got to him in the end. Furthermore, he knew it, thus his choice of the rope." Satisfied with his assessment of the situation, the Dean topped up Professor Trout's glass and turned the discussion to the Education Minister's unseemly, hasty departure, his politician's fear of scandal having quickly superseded his earlier avant-garde posturing.

"Seen it all before," the Dean said with the same certainty and inaccuracy which he had applied to McNally. "It's the Icarus syndrome. As a result of today's fiasco I make two predictions. First that that fool of an Education Minister is off the scene within a month; and second and more important, so too will be the Vice-Chancellor and we will soon be back to the old order."

And consistent as always when it came to life's realities, the Dean of Humanities was wrong.

CHAPTER FIFTEEN

cNALLY'S SUICIDE, if an unfortunate beginning to the university's much-vaunted installation art ambitions, otherwise induced no mourning. The Vice-Chancellor acted quickly, transferring an elderly Chaucer professor to the stage-design lectureship, and normality was restored.

In the mediaeval philosophy department Professor Trout was hard at work writing Frewen's conference speech. He put down his pen and reread his opening draft text.

I stand before you today both proud and humble – humble as a male at your open-minded and generous acceptance of my participation in this noble associated discipline in the vital arena of women's scholarship, and proud to play a role, albeit modest, in pioneering a new and long-overdue academic epistemology.

I willingly abandoned a successful journalism career to serve under the remarkable Professor Beefenstein, a scholar whose erudition has attracted national attention and for whom I have the greatest admiration, motivated by my realization that Rubenesque Studies represents all the finest virtues we universally aspire to in the twenty-first century.

I refer to democracy and its underlying spirit of egalitarianism and fairness. I refer to integrity in accepting reality as nature intended and in turn, acknowledging its fundamental innate beauty; and most of all, I refer to human dignity and mutual respect.

For too long western women have tolerated cruel social pressures contrived by profiteering commercial interests who, wittingly or otherwise, reflect in their mendacious actions the very opposite of the virtues I have mentioned, namely undemocratic elitism, unfairness, dishonesty and disrespect.

Good conference speech opening bumf, the Professor thought to himself, pleased with what he had so far written. Better bung in the first joke about here, he decided. Frewen would be nervous and would need a positive audience response early to encourage him. But Good God, a joke to this audience presented serious problems. The Professor had heard about Women's Studies types – aggressive, mean-spirited, frequently embittered lesbians, humourless, intellectually shallow and, reputedly, very ugly. He would need to be careful. The joke must obviously be at men's expense and carry a fairly vicious sting. And in plain language too, he reflected. Any subtlety might be over the heads of this audience.

Then there was the body of the address to consider. That would certainly be a problem. He had read the Berkeley

Women's Studies textbooks Frewen had delivered, and been dismayed by their contents, or more particularly their total lack of meaningful substance.

The opening chapters, with titles such as Is Women's Studies an Academic Discipline?, were a giveaway in their implicit need for justification. The substance of the primers was simply verbose nonsense. Forty years of essay-marking and thesis-reading had developed in the Professor a keen eye for meaningless rubbish camouflaged by unnecessary big words, esoteric tangents, straw-men targets and all of the standard fraudulent gimmicks applied by non-academic poseurs.

Thank God it was a conference, the Professor thought. After the first two minutes most of the audience would have turned off, regardless of what was being said, and the post-address applause would strictly reflect the shortness of the speech and the delegates' gratitude at its completion.

He battled on, devised two anti-men jokes, the second and better to conclude the address with, and by 3pm he was finished and it was in his typist's hands. Professor Trout then telephoned Frewen and instructed him to come over to pick up the speech.

It was six weeks since he'd last seen Frewen, who had warily stayed away following the blast directed at him on the last occasion they had met, and since then a three-week term break had passed. The Professor was taken aback by his appearance.

Frewen had blown up enormously. Clearly he was unable to do his jacket button up and his belly bulged before him, while his face, puffy at the outset, was now set in rolling jowls, only partly hidden by the commencement of his beard.

"I see you have begun your weight-increment empathy programme," the Professor remarked casually.

"It's all this intellectual fine-tuning I've been doing marking essays that's done it Prof," Frewen explained. "Sharpens the old mind no end, I can tell you, but just ends up causing trouble."

"Well, Mr Frewen, you do surprise me. Hitherto I laboured under the belief that development of one's mental faculties was unrelated to corpulence."

"No, Prof. Wrong end of the stick. Give you an example. Two Sundays ago I went to the zoo. Anyway, there I was…"

"The zoo?" Professor Trout exclaimed. "Again you surprise me, Mr Frewen. Frankly, I would not have suspected you possessed an interest in fauna – animals," he added hurriedly, noticing Frewen's puzzlement.

"Quite right, Prof. Not really my forté, animals. Not since I was married to the Irish waitress, that is. Quite put me off animals that did, I can tell you."

Professor Trout frowned. "That's surely a trifle severe, Mr Frewen. Your wife's ancestry may raise some concerns but to deny her essential humanity is …"

Frewen interrupted. "It was her murdering Horace that did it for me," he said darkly.

Professor Trout started, "Well of course I wasn't aware of that. I'm shocked to hear of it. Your marriage termination obviously becomes more explicable in those circumstances."

"I loved that bird," Frewen muttered sorrowfully.

"I see," Professor Trout said flatly. "I presume she's incarcerated. Doubtless she will be released in due course and perhaps you can pick up where …"

"No, not her, Prof," Frewen said impatiently. "My budgie, Horace. Strangled him, she did. Claimed his chirping made her morning hangovers worse. I've never been able to relate to animals since then."

There was a pause while the Professor allowed this confusing information to fall into place. "So why the zoo?" he eventually asked.

"Damned partner made me go with her. She had her eight-year-old niece down from Chester for the weekend. Anyway, when we reached the elephant enclosure the sign said elephants were the largest creatures on earth and because of their size they have no natural enemies. Lo and behold, flash, the old light-bulb went off in my head. Like I said, it's all this intellectual fine-tuning that's done it. Would never have occurred to me in my journalism days, I can tell you."

"I'm sorry," the now-baffled Professor said. "I don't understand."

"It was like this, Prof. First thing on Monday I bailed up the old Beefenstein and told her I'd had a brainwave. Elephants are the largest animals on earth, I said, and their size means they have no natural enemies. Well, Beefy got really excited. Told me I was developing into an outstanding scholar. Said I'd opened up an entirely new course topic in defence of Rubenesquism, namely the evidence of nature, and that she would take it over and write it all up. She said I'd come up with this new intellectual breakthrough just in time. Bit of a relief, actually. Two days before my elephant discovery Beefy sent me a note saying next year I had to lecture on eco-feminism. It's another new course she's invented. I was going to ask you to explain what it is."

"I'm pleased to say I have no idea, Mr Frewen. Nor do I wish to find out."

"No worries, Prof. Beefy's dropped it now, thanks to my discovery. She said she was unhappy about it anyway as it didn't involve sizeism. Instead we're doing the whole third year on what she calls Size-meritism Studies. Never seen her so excited. She's knocked up one course on the animal food chain – you know, how little animals get eaten by bigger buggers and so on up. The biggest wins, which proves being big is good, she says. 'Nother one she's come up with thanks to my elephant brainwave is how humans, as the most intelligent species, always show more respect for animals the bigger they are – you know, Prof, save the whales and all that carry-on. 'Nother one is …"

"I don't want to hear any more, thank you Mr Frewen. However, your professor does appear to have overlooked the public's affection for kittens and puppies, not to mention hamsters, pet rabbits and – if you will forgive my raising it – budgies and other birds."

Frewen looked alarmed. "Good Lord, Prof, you're right. You won't tell her, will you? See Professor, next year our first batch of degree-course fat girls go into their third year and we've run out of topics to do workshops on. Beefy thought she'd find the answer last week when four New Zealand fat women visited us. Enormous they were, right up there in Beefy's league. Seems over there they've got a Ministry of Women's Affairs and they were from that outfit."

"I find the possibility of such an agency highly improbable, Mr Frewen."

"Know what you mean Prof, but that's what Beefy said. She claimed this New Zealand Women's Affairs Department has been going for about fifteen years and she was hoping they'd give her some ideas for the third-year courses."

"I see," Professor Trout said. "And did they?"

"That's the whole point, Prof. That's why Beefy was so pleased with my scientific discovery. Turned out they'd flown all the way from New Zealand, first class too – they were bragging about that because they wouldn't fit into normal seats. They came specially to visit us, hoping we'd give them some ideas. Seems they've spent the past fifteen years trying to think up what to do themselves and they thought we'd have the answers, so you can see why I'm the golden-haired boy for a change."

"My congratulations, Mr Frewen," Professor Trout said. "Your scholarship is certainly impressive. So I take it your point in gaining all this weight is to emulate the survival example set by elephants?"

"No, no, wrong end of the stick; on the elephant front that is, but that's what Beefy said too, about my scholarship." Frewen frowned. "That's the bloody problem. I'm not too sure about becoming too damned sharp. Suddenly Beefy's taking a real interest in me; treating me seriously as a Rubenesque scholar if you get my drift, and wanting me to come up with more intellectual ideas. It's all very well for her, but the old brain needs a bit of a rest after that sort of effort with the elephants. Now it's personal bloody supervision on the weight empathy front. Damned woman's made me join her for three meals a day in the university cafeteria. I can't even choose them. Breakfast is six sausages, bacon, chips, four fried eggs and six slices of toast, lunch is …"

"I don't think I want to hear those details, Mr Frewen," the Professor said. "Here's your speech. You might need to make copies for each delegate. Ask Professor Beefenstein, as it may well be that the conference organizers will deal with producing copies. You must read the address at least a dozen times so you're familiar with it, and also practise its delivery in front of the mirror." The Professor tendered this advice conscious that Frewen would struggle with some of the deliberately chosen big words, included to impress the delegates.

"You've saved my life, Professor," Frewen gushed. "I've been panicking for weeks. Thought maybe me and you were history after our last meeting, and I was planning to swear off ill. I'd even telephoned a bloke I once knew, Dr Ali up in Sheffield. He's got a bloody mortgage on the local illicit abortion market. Always been decent to me after I didn't write him up like I was 'sposed to. He sent me some pills to take which he promised would put me in hospital for a safe three days. He said, no worries, I wouldn't feel anything, I'd be laughing …"

"Yes, well that won't be necessary now," Professor Trout interrupted. "Just make sure you reread the address several times."

Suddenly Frewen paled. "Christ, that means now I'll have to lead the bloody protest on Thursday. I was going to take the pills on Wednesday night to get out of that too."

"Protest? What protest?"

"Outside the Health Office over their anti-obesity campaign. Beefy says I have to be arrested. She says it will establish my credentials for the conference. She's already teed up the newspapers and television. I fear the poo, Professor."

"I rather think your concerns are unfounded," Professor Trout said. "I suspect your professor's sentiments about your impending arrest and possible temporary incarceration will be emphatically shared by the Vice-Chancellor."

"A good career move, you think?" Frewen enquired cautiously.

"In your field, indisputably," Professor Trout replied and then: "Have you made a start on your pamphlet – you know, your bibliography build-up? If I recall correctly you were going to set your students essays on heart-attack mythology to yield up some material."

Frewen saddened. "Took your advice, Prof, and did it. Problem was all the essays were more or less the same. No graphs or anything, if you get my drift. Just all going on about thin uncles who had died of heart attacks and that sort of thing."

"So?"

"No meat in it, Prof. I mean, what could I copy?"

Professor Trout, a lifetime's politeness causing him to choose his words carefully, responded, "I believe in the broad field of social science it is not uncommon practice to publish what are generally described as case histories." Noting Frewen's puzzlement, he elaborated. "I understand that reproducing a series of case studies, no matter how repetitive, is considered acceptable scholarship in the social sciences, Mr Frewen. The fact of their commonality is deemed to reinforce the underlying point."

Frewen adopted a strained expression. "I'll give it a bit of thought then, Prof. Right now I need a rest after the elephant effort. Never pays to rush these things and not get it right. Learnt that in journalism. Golden rule there. Less is more – know what I mean?"

"A prudent policy, Mr Frewen. Now I'm afraid I must leave you as I'm going out this evening. But please ensure you return next week and tell me all about the conference."

But Frewen was not finished. "Rode on an elephant once I did, Prof," he declared solemnly.

"Is that right? Not I presume in India," the Professor teased.

"No, no. Not India. M' Gran took me to the zoo when I was ten. Thing is, I've been wondering if my elephant breakthrough could have been one of those subconscious things, and not just the old mind sharpened now I'm out of journalism. Whatta you think, Prof?"

"Well, you did mention you read a sign containing

your breakthrough information, Mr Frewen, which rather eliminates the subconscious from consideration."

"But that's the thing, Prof!" Frewen cried. "If I was still a journalist I wouldn't have twigged to the connection even if I had read it. Riding that elephant had quite an effect on me, I can tell you."

"Perhaps then a mixture of the subconscious heightened by your sharpened scholar's mind," the Professor suggested.

"Right, Prof. That's pretty much the way I see it." And on that note of accord the meeting was terminated.

CHAPTER SIXTEEN

PROFESSOR TROUT WAS indeed going out: to celebrate, in fact. He had reserved a table at the town's
best restaurant and Enid and he were intending to toast the
new life awaiting them.

For as it transpired Enid had readily agreed to the St
Andrews proposal, indeed she had expressed surprising
enthusiasm and had promptly taken control of the required
planning. Dealing with an estate agent, she had organized
a three-year lease of their house to one of the new Ralston
academics, the professor for the proposed new Private
Detectives School, having first secured assurance from the
agent as to his suitability. "Excellent credentials. Twenty years
in the police as a detective, then tossed out for corruption," the
estate agent had said. "An ideal tenant. He'll be most anxious
to keep his nose clean on every front."

For his part, Professor Trout had flown to Edinburgh, been

picked up at the airport by Walter King and after driving to St Andrews and depositing his bags at his hotel, he had spent a delightful day at the university.

The Dean of Humanities, Professor John Feast, had greeted him effusively and thanked him for allowing publication of his book, then that evening, together with a small group of academics chosen by King, hosted a dinner party in an elegant private dining room at the town's most prestigious hotel. It was quickly apparent to Professor Trout that the principal reason for the dinner was to persuade him to join them, so he wasted no time and during the pre-dinner drinks made it clear that he was looking forward to doing so. There were handshakes and congratulations, then Professor Feast proposed a toast to Professor Trout. It was all highly gratifying after the past year.

Before they sat down, Professor Trout, supported by Walter King, described to much astonishment the developments at Ralston.

Encouraged by the awareness of common ground and emboldened by a third glass of wine, Professor Trout then raised the criticisms of the Humanities faculty which had been advanced months earlier by Professor Bayley, the Science Dean at Ralston, for they had weighed heavily on his mind ever since.

"That's a foolish approach," Professor Feast said dismissively. "Even if he's correct in asserting that we have been lax – and it is a point of view I do not concede – it is the huge advances in science in recent years which compound the need for the humanities: that is, to put meaning to it all. Additionally, I hardly need detail the many serious concerns arising from scientific developments: concerns which raise enormous moral, ethical, environmental and social issues and which more than ever before necessitate students of history and philosophy to provide perspective – if, that is, society is not to make some ghastly blunders. I do not disdain the scientists: rather, I acknowledge our respective roles. Theirs to find the facts; ours to weigh them and make judgements. We are mutually dependent."

"I suspect Professor Bayley would not take kindly to that inferior boffin role, especially with us as the sages," Professor Trout remarked.

"Then I haven't explained it properly," Feast replied. "I'm not suggesting a lesser status for science. Neither stands above the other: rather, each complements the other. Ideally, our humanities students would undertake some science and mathematics studies and likewise the reverse for science and mathematics scholars. But the important point is that we are teachers, not practitioners. It's for our students, once out in the world, and not for us, to apply the wisdom they hopefully derive from their humanities studies. In some respects our role as humanities academics is the modern equivalent of the mediaeval priest – that is, essentially contemplative."

"So you don't share Professor Bayley's view that we should have a public profile beyond the university?" Professor Trout asked.

"No I do not," Feast said. "We are work-horses, not

show-ponies. The academic writing populist books for an audience beyond his own teaching sphere, or presenting radio or television programmes on science, wildlife or politics, is at heart a showman. Nothing wrong with that, but he's in the wrong field and invariably ends up where he really desires to be – that is, as a public figure: politician, current-affairs television presenter or serious journalist."

"I certainly agree that in a perfect world all science, law and other serious students should first complete a humanities degree as a solid knowledge foundation to build their specialisation on," a history professor proffered.

"They actually did once," King said. "It was common practice in the nineteenth century."

"It was the case with law students too, up to half a century ago," the poetry professor said. "Plus they had to take Roman Law and Latin as compulsory subjects."

"That's why our prisons are nowadays filled with delinquent lawyers," Feast laughed. "Never used to happen in the old days. Back then a law degree was virtually a certificate of respectability; now it's seen as the badge of a wide-boy, and with good cause. But all of that aside, the root of the problem lies in excessive specialization. It's as simple as that, and precisely why we need humanities generalists to neutralize the dangers accruing from it."

Professor Trout recounted the Ralston Science Dean's rationalization for turning a blind eye to the nonsense courses because of the funding benefits.

"I suppose it's a question of where you draw the line," Feast said. "In some respects we're just as guilty here at St Andrews with our media studies and commerce courses."

"There's quite a gulf between those and astrology," the poetry professor argued.

"Yes, but the principle's the same in terms of a university being an institution of knowledge and scholarship," Feast persisted. "After all, our largest faculty is commerce, simply pumping out MBA dullards. My brother-in-law explained it all to me. He's the CEO of Scotland's second-biggest bank. He said an MBA is a certificate of sober intent and ordinariness: just the sort of unimaginative clods needed for middle management, to carry out but never initiate policies. He claimed it's analogous to the army. An MBA possessor is essentially cannon-fodder, at best about the equivalent of an officer never to be promoted beyond a major. Anyway, the issue's academic. It's too late to turn the clock back now."

Listening to all of this made Professor Trout slightly ashamed that he had not made the same seemingly obvious points to Professor Bayley, but nevertheless, when he sat down to dine he felt a contentment which had been absent from his life for the past two years.

A most enjoyable debate had arisen over Kantian influence on Scottish devolution and later in the evening, a ferocious row erupted over the merits of Philip Larkin's poetry. It was all as Professor Trout joyfully recalled from his earlier academic years, and the Larkin debate in particular had left a mark, standing in stark contrast to his last meeting with the Vice-Chancellor when he had called to complain about the re-employment of the Ralston mediaeval philosophy librarians as cleaners.

"Only positions available at present, so you must not think I'm picking on your department, Professor," the Vice-Chancellor had said. "Believe me, you're well down the pecking order of the reform targets." His face had darkened. "Do you realise, Professor, this university has a poetry department? And if that's not outrageous enough, a poetry department with six staff – six, I tell you – and a mere 29 students – if, that is, poetry can be deemed a topic of study. It's scandalous parasitism such as I've never seen, and viewed in the wider context of my mandate from the Council going forward, I can assure you I intend stamping out this racket. Never heard such nonsense. It's plumbers not poets the world needs. I ask you: who reads poetry? Who employs a poet? What use is poetry to anyone?"

"Strange as it may seem, many people read poetry," the Professor responded sardonically. "They've done so for over two thousand years and doubtless will continue to in the future. I hesitate to say this to you but it's part of our cultural tradition."

"Ah!" the Vice-Chancellor declared triumphantly. "Got you there, haven't I? I should have seen culture coming. I'm afraid you're living in the past, Professor Turbot. Modern students are not in the least interested in that sort of airy-fairy culture guff. They have their feet firmly on the ground, mark my words, and all credit to them. It's a new age, Professor: an age of realism, and this university intends aligning itself with that and being in the forefront of the new practical thinking going forward. You should bear in mind that before accepting this position I spent a full uninterrupted ten days reading up on universities, so I think I may modestly claim a degree of expertise, if not indeed, authority, on the subject of higher education."

"I certainly bow to your expertise, given that study," the Professor mocked, then, more seriously, "Personally I think it's a tragedy. You're denying students an all-important foundation to their education."

"Not the way modern students see it, I'm afraid," the Vice-Chancellor replied airily. "They have a far more pragmatic approach. They do not view education as an end in itself – that's old-fashioned thinking. To the contrary, they see higher education as an unavoidable hurdle to be surmounted as quickly as possible so they can get on the starting block in life's race – a necessary evil in fact; rather like going to the dentist. You have only to consider the absence of objections when I built over the cricket ground to rehouse the humanities faculty. To be candid, Professor, I admit I anticipated complaints. Well let me tell you, I received only four – all members of the university's cricket team and ..." his face darkened – "all conspicuously humanities students. I'm pleased to say the days of attending universities to gallivant about, playing games and talking infantile nonsense into the night about politics and religion and all that sort of time-wasting rubbish, are long gone and we shall certainly embrace this new spirit at Ralston going forward."

"Talking nonsense into the night, as you put it, about

politics and religion, is one of the most important functions for students attending universities," Professor Trout argued. "It is a vital part of a student's personal development in cultivating their thinking and weighing issues in wider contexts, it ..."

"Rubbish!" the Vice-Chancellor exploded. "May have been the case once but where did it get anyone? Nowhere, that's where! I blame all that garbage for the sixties and seventies socialism. The universities turned out a lot of clever-speak wastrels with arts degrees in poetry and the other useless stuff. Weren't capable of making a living, so they talked the powers-that-be into giving them useless sinecures. Made everyone else pay for them doing bogus jobs in unnecessary government agencies. Well, mark my words, Professor Fish, those days are well and truly over! The modern student wants to whip through university as quickly as he can then get out into the real world and make a living."

"A degree factory, you mean," the Professor snorted. "Why not just sell them degrees and save them the bother of coming here at all?"

But his sarcasm was lost on the Vice-Chancellor. "Not a practical suggestion," he said ruefully. "Unfortunately, most students don't have any money and are reliant on grants so we're obliged to go through the motions of lecture courses. I'll be frank with you, Professor. Student poverty is a fundamental commercial flaw in the university business, which is why we're actively pursuing a programme of supplementary revenue sources. Were those alternative finance options not available I have no doubt we would close down all universities, as it would be the economically rational decision to make."

Realizing he was wasting his time, Professor Trout had left; thus when three weeks later he had returned from Scotland elated, he had happily written out his resignation and personally delivered it to the Vice-Chancellor.

"Excellent," the Vice-Chancellor declared after quickly scanning it. "Glad you've seen the light and are doing the sensible thing. We must move with the times. I shall close the mediaeval philosophy department at the end of this year."

"But my lecturers!" Professor Trout protested. "I was intending to propose Margaret Clark succeed me as Professor. She has first-rate …"

"Please, please, Professor," the Vice-Chancellor said, raising his hands. "Be assured we will happily reassign your lecturers. The university is flourishing. We're in desperate need of staff with the undoubted teaching skills your lecturers have under their belts. One has only to look at Mr Frewen's success in adjusting to see that the difficulties with such transitions are largely imaginary. He is an example to everyone with his fine spirit of co-operation and is indisputably a man of the future here at Ralston. Matter of fact, and I'm certainly happy to respect your judgement, I see no reason why your lecturers, assuming they adopt the example set by Mr Frewen, should not both become professors – in new disciplines of course," he added hastily. "With the appropriate salary increments, naturally."

"Such as?"

"I invite you to open your mind, Professor, and not leap

to hasty judgement. Are you aware how many hamburgers are consumed annually?"

Professor Trout looked puzzled. "I beg your pardon?" he said.

"Fourteen billion worldwide, Professor. Billion, not million – billion. That, I assure you, is the greatest academic window of opportunity I've yet encountered. Fourteen billion! It defies belief that such a significant element of contemporary life has remained unnoticed by academia, and reveals just how out of touch with life's realities universities have become. On the other hand, it provides an excellent opportunity for Ralston. We're starting a one-year diploma course in hamburgerology and our consultants' preliminary survey claims we'll achieve a commencing roll of 200 pupils, rising over three years to 750. The education authorities have been most supportive. It's a splendid opportunity for your staff to embrace an entirely new field."

Professor Trout was, to say the least, not a violent man. There had been a single incident when he was twelve which had led to a brief scuffle with another boy over the disputed ownership of a pencil. It had been instantly terminated by a teacher and thereafter the Professor had existed without a single experience of emotionally prompted physicality. He had always reacted with puzzlement to the regular newspaper accounts of violent behaviour, with much the same incomprehension he'd have felt if Martians had appeared before him. But now, for the first time in his sixty-four years, he felt an unfamiliar urge to tip the Vice-Chancellor's desk over or smash a window

– anything, just so long as it was violent.

The Vice-Chancellor, a veteran of such responses, quickly detected the vibes. "These proposals will naturally be a matter of discussion with your lecturers, Professor Trout," he said quickly. "It may well be that they are uncomfortable with such modernism; and if so then we can explore alternatives," and the Professor's unfamiliar impulse began to wane.

In the event, three months later, although by then beyond the knowledge of the now-departed Professor Trout who was happily ensconced at St Andrews, the two mediaeval philosophy lecturers both became professors: Jon Johansson the Professor of Upholstery and Margaret Clark Professor of Panelbeating, this office having remained vacant since Frewen's departure.

CHAPTER SEVENTEEN

PROFESSOR TROUT HAD two months remaining at the university, his home for the past 38 years. But his melancholy at the fate that had befallen Ralston had lately moved to a mixture of relief at leaving and optimism at his impending transfer to the St Andrews academic environment.

He now viewed the Vice-Chancellor's modernization programme with resigned bemusement, although the commencement of the School of Paedophiliac Studies in the adjacent space of his barracks was a dismaying factor. The visual blot of outsized roly-polys seen from his former study window had been replaced in the new premises by shabbily dressed middle-aged men who moved about furtively, avoiding all eye contact. Visits by policemen and detectives were a regular event, often culminating in one of the paedophilia scholars being taken away, head downcast and handcuffed to a policeman carrying videos confiscated from the School.

"Early days yet," the Vice-Chancellor confided cheerfully to the Professor when he called unexpectedly to inspect the new humanities premises. "Mostly unfrocked priests and scoutmasters enrolled so far, but I have great faith in our consultants' report on the potential market once the word gets out. Apparently paedophilia scholars have embraced modern technology to an impressive degree – just the sort of forward-looking students we want. I'm reliably informed that on their own initiative they've established global networks for research purposes on the internet, thereby allowing us to pinpoint target our promotional activity."

Professor Trout complained about the regular police visits and arrests. "Yes, I'm fully aware of that," the Vice-Chancellor said angrily. "It's quite disgraceful. The affected scholars have assured me the charges made against them are complete misunderstandings. They've been subject to all sorts of vile accusations when – as they've quite reasonably pointed out – all they were engaged in was innocent practical research, essential for their field of study. It's an intolerable state of affairs, tantamount to censorship, and I have lodged a complaint with the police."

Despite the paedophilia department, given his pending departure, Professor Trout remained in good spirits and it was in such a mood that he greeted gleefully the *Telegraph*'s photograph in the home news section on the Friday morning before the weekend of the Cologne Women's Studies conference. For pictured centre-page was Frewen, his fear-ridden bladderish face bulging as he struggled in the grasp of two straining policemen who were being pummelled by a heaving herd of mountainous Rubenesque Studies students.

The *Telegraph* reported this in a frivolous tone with the heading WEIGHTY PROTEST AT WHITEHALL, while its supporting article began: "Two policemen were heavied yesterday …" and went on to describe the demonstration in a similarly facetious manner. Frewen, it transpired, had spent the night in the cells and was scheduled to appear in court that morning on assault charges.

A head-shot of Professor Beefenstein was shown with an accompanying story quoting her, to the obvious although obliquely expressed amusement of the *Telegraph* writer, describing Frewen as a great social reformer and a martyr for justice whose name would be forever etched in the annals of liberation causes. A further protest outside the court was promised for today.

The Professor picked up his other daily, the *Guardian*, and was delighted to see they had accorded the event twice as much coverage, and on their front page. Unlike the *Telegraph*, the *Guardian* reported the event sympathetically, their heading reading POLICE SMASH CRY FOR JUSTICE. A statement attributed to Frewen was included, which the Professor recognized as clearly beyond his competence and which he correctly assumed must have been written by Professor Beefenstein. It began with an assurance that he intended devoting his life to the cause of justice for women, for he could no longer ignore their plight arising from the artifice and oppression of manipulative commercial interests. There was a great deal more in this vein and Professor Trout's delight overflowed when further on he discovered the *Guardian* had accorded its second leader to the affair. "Time For Truth-Telling", the editorial was headed. It read:

> The peaceful demonstration brutally crushed by the police in London yesterday is a wake-up call to all Britons and in particular to men, rather than reliance on our long-suffering womenfolk to carry the flag of reform.
>
> Unbounded admiration must be extended to the activist academic Frewen who has boldly shaken our lethargy in ignoring for so long the outrageous pressures placed on women to conform, contrary to the only laws that count being those of nature, to an idealised interpretation of women's bodies.
>
> The clarion call sounded by the energetic Mr Frewen yesterday will hopefully echo across the land and resonate in the mind of every citizen. The burden of pursuing the truth must not be solely shouldered by courageous intellectuals such as Mr Frewen, in seeking the long overdue union of natural justice with nature.
>
> We unhesitantly endorse …

Professor Trout read the accounts with increasing joy, then, remembering he had a meeting with the Vice-Chancellor that morning, sought at the latter's request, he instructed Enid to keep the newspapers so that he might enjoy rereading them again that evening, and he left for the university.

For the first time he was greeted warmly by the Vice-

Chancellor, who was in an exuberant mood. "Delighted to see you, Professor Trout," he gushed, and instructed his secretary to bring in coffee, another first.

"Seen the newspapers?" he enthused, rubbing his hands together. "Splendid publicity! Splendid! Can't put a price on it. It will place Ralston firmly on the academic map. Mark my words: we'll be knocked over by enrolments for Rubenesque Studies. I can envisage a time when it may well be our principal field of scholarship, at least as reflected by student numbers, which would certainly testify we're on the right educational path. I'm a great believer in healthy competition, Professor. The race between the Astrology, Rubenesque Studies and Grief Counselling departments to become the largest in student numbers provides precisely the type of intellectually stimulating climate one seeks in a modern university. And there's quite a few others showing promise which will give them a run for their money. The line-dancing diploma course has now passed ninety enrolments and the African Drumming, Puppetry and Yoga departments are all bursting at the seams. Aside from those enrolment benefits, on the intellectual front Frewen and his students have demonstrated just how much a progressive university can achieve: change people's thinking, teach them to open their minds and embrace new concepts. We should all be very proud of them."

"I take it you do not subscribe to Dr Johnson's view that a university is a place where students come to learn, not to teach?" Professor Trout asked drily.

"Dr Johnson?" The Vice-Chancellor searched his mind.

"Can't say I know him. But who's he to comment, anyway? He should stick to medicine and not comment on academic matters beyond his competence."

Professor Trout decided not to elaborate. "So you're quite happy about Frewen's arrest?" he enquired.

"Happy? I'm not happy, Professor Trout: I'm euphoric! Furthermore it's a double-whammy. We'll enjoy another round of first-rate publicity after today's court hearing." Suddenly he frowned. "Mind you, not altogether perfectly planned, unfortunately. Pity it's a Friday. That's a low newspaper readership and television viewing day. Then again, I don't suppose academics can be expected to know about that sort of thing," he added ruefully.

"Oh? Why's that?" Professor Trout enquired curiously.

"Always a giveaway in commerce and politics, Professor. If you have bad news to announce then Friday's your day. No-one pays much attention to the news, for some reason, on Fridays. The Rubenesque Studies protest at Whitehall should have been earlier in the week, dammit!"

"Well it's not all bad," Professor Trout suggested helpfully. "You'll have newspaper coverage of the court hearing tomorrow."

The Vice-Chancellor brightened. "Excellent point, Professor! An added bonus, on reflection. Saturday's big for newspaper readership. Oh, the enrolments, the enrolments!" he cried, again rubbing his hands together. "There's no doubt about our debt to Frewen," he enthused. "I can envisage students across the land clamouring to switch universities and join Ralston.

They've had nothing to march about since the Vietnam war."
His face darkened. "Well there was Thatcherism. Bad business
that: protesting about Margaret. Quite disgraceful. But you know
the score, Professor. Your average student sometimes likes to think
of himself as a revolutionary. Sticking up posters of Che Guevara
in their rooms is all very well as far as it goes, but hardly satisfies
the necessary civil disobedience yearning of young people on
the verge of maturity; and they lack the imagination to think
up things themselves to contrive rage about. Frewen's call to
arms is a master-stroke. I'm seriously thinking of commissioning
posters of him and distributing them nationwide. You know the
sort of thing: a lightly sketched illustration of him with a halo
above his head, leading the masses into battle as it were, holding
a red flag aloft and with the other arm pointing into the future
– promised land, liberation, all that sort of imagery which young
people respond so well to. He's had the initiative to grow a beard
as well and certainly looks the part. I can see Frewen becoming
a cult figure, which will do wonders for enrolments. I'm going
to tie him into a long-term contract before he's grabbed by one
of our rivals. What do you think, Professor?"

"It sounds very new-Ralston. I shall certainly look forward
to seeing the poster. But perhaps canonization could be a little
excessive. May I suggest instead, an aura of light about Mr
Frewen's head."

"Delighted you endorse the poster idea, Professor. You've
been in the academic world longer than me and I certainly
respect your judgement about the presentation. I'll take your
advice and get on to it smartly."

Professor Trout decided to ignore this assumption. "You wanted to see me, Vice-Chancellor?"

"Yes, yes, so I did," the Vice-Chancellor said dreamily; but his mind remained fixed on Frewen's triumph. "Of course we'll have to do something about his current status," he mused. "In the circumstances it would be totally inappropriate for Frewen to remain a junior lecturer. He's a man on the move and epitomises the new academic environment we seek going forward. I don't see why we can't leap a rung and make him a senior lecturer and then take it from there. We're going to need a considerable staff build-up in that department, and he's the one with the established scholarship credentials. It's merit that counts in the modern world, Professor Trout, not the outmoded time-serving old way of thinking." The Vice-Chancellor lolled back in his seat, his hands clasped across his middle. "I'm beginning to understand why Frewen abandoned journalism," he said. "In my previous careers I had considerable contact with the media, and can speak with some authority when I say journalists are not noted for their character or vision. Frewen would have been a square peg in a round hole in that world, but here at Ralston he's plainly found his natural vocation. There's no doubt he's entitled to promotion."

"That certainly sounds an excellent idea. I'm sure Mr Frewen will be delighted," Professor Trout said, eager to advance the folly.

"Of course, far be it for me to seek acclamation for discovering Frewen," the Vice-Chancellor continued. "But I do claim a little credit on a different count, namely that his success is confirmation of my belief – which regrettably has met with a decidedly belligerent and unreasonable response from many of your redundant humanities colleagues – that tutoring ability in one discipline is readily transferable to others." Again his face darkened. "Just look at that," he complained, pointing to a broken window Professor Trout had hitherto not noticed. "One of your associates, I'm afraid: Professor Munz, the history fellow. Quite disgraceful behaviour, specially for a man of his years. I made a perfectly reasonable proposal regarding two of his lecturers who have to go – offered excellent positions in the new Department of Alternative Medicine – and there's your result. He put on a preposterous tantrum, then threw my pyrex pyramid I was showing him through the window. The newly appointed alternative medicine professor presented it to me. Promised it would prevent cancer."

"You certainly don't want to lose it then," Professor Trout teased.

The Vice-Chancellor became pensive. "You know, Professor Trout, you may think I'm a bit of a stick-in-the-mud; call me sentimental, even soft if you will, but I do deplore the loss of old-fashioned values: of courtesy and politeness and, in the case of Professor Munz and his lecturers, of simple gratitude. One goes out of one's way to accommodate redundant employees – something I might add which is contrary to all best practice in my previous company receivership career – only to be subject to shameful conduct like that," and again he indicated the broken window. "It's totally reprehensible," he grumbled.

"Oh, I don't know," Professor Trout said provocatively.

"You must remember Professor Munz's professional life has been imbued with violence – history sometimes seems to be nothing less. In the circumstances he probably acted with considerable restraint."

"Never thought of it in that context," the Vice-Chancellor said grudgingly. "Dangerous man, is he? I appreciate your warning and will certainly be careful dealing with him in future. Still, given that I was trying to assist with his staff reassignments, I don't think it's excusable; and aside from that, you'd think a man of his age would be particularly interested in medical matters."

"Professor Munz strikes me as a man enjoying rude health, Vice-Chancellor. I suspect that rather supports the probability that he leans towards conventional medical practice."

"A narrow attitude, Professor," the Vice-Chancellor responded sharply. "Don't mean it insultingly of course – had the same problems myself initially in opening my mind to fresh concepts outside the square. It came home to me particularly strongly after we adopted the consultants' advice and introduced our Witchcraft Department. We had 48 student enrolments in the first term and it all ended unhappily. We researched what was wrong – a fundamental error by us – me indeed, I imagine you're thinking, and rightly so: I take full responsibility. But equally, it was also I who worked out the solution. Did my own homework. What I discovered was that our witchcraft scholars weren't interested in the discipline in any historic sense, and there I can certainly sympathize. Difficult to imagine a more useless subject than history. No:

their interest lay solely in practising the art. We pulled in the nuclear physics lecturer – the peace crowd lot had destroyed the market for his stuff – and we promoted him to Professor of Witchcraft."

"I can't believe what I'm hearing," Professor Trout muttered.

"Ah, that's because you don't know the full story," the Vice-Chancellor replied smugly. "Simple matter really. As I said, we dropped all the witchcraft history stuff – quite right too – as I said, who cares about the past: it's the present people are interested in. Once we changed the name to the Department of Applied Witchcraft enrolments shot up. We now have 110 applied witchcraft scholars. Why? Because we were giving them subjects they wanted to engage in – not endless babble about silly history but actually practising witchcraft – and all credit to the former nuclear physics lecturer for grasping the nettle."

Professor Trout began to worry. Plainly his mediaeval philosophy lecturers' re-assignments were the reason for the meeting. "Is that what you wished to see me about?" he enquired tentatively, bracing himself for the expected preposterous proposals.

"No, no, not at all," the Vice-Chancellor said hurriedly. "No, the matter I wish to discuss, Professor Trout, is your students, now we're closing your department down. Are you aware that four of your first-year students and three of your second-year students are majoring in mediaeval philosophy? Quite extraordinary," he muttered in an undertone to himself.

"Of course I am."

"I see. Well, unfortunately a small problem has arisen. You have a student called Angela Somerset. I think she might be black."

"So she is; but if you don't know her, what makes you think that?"

"Well, her father's black – so it occurred to me she possibly could be."

"I see," the Professor said wryly. "You will find with black people that's not an uncommon tendency. They can sometimes be a bit strange that way."

Ignoring the Professor's sarcasm the Vice-Chancellor barked, "Troublemaker, is she?"

"Troublemaker? Most certainly not: to the contrary in fact. She's an extremely clever young lady. We're rather pleased with her. Miss Somerset is an exceptional student and has made an outstanding contribution to discussion. I can't imagine how she could be a problem."

"Well actually she's not. It's her damned father, Basil Somerset. Heard of him, have you?"

"No. Should I have?"

The Vice-Chancellor looked troubled. "Look here," he said. "Just between you and me and inside these four walls, I'm damn sure bloody Somerset is out to cause havoc. He's a rather aggressive barrister. He acted for some trade unions in a stand-off I had when disposing of a workforce in my old job a few years back. Never forgiven me over the workers' wages not being paid, and now he thinks he has me over a barrel.

He's talking about suing the university for pulling stumps on your thing; you know ..." the Vice-Chancellor hesitated, then remembered – "mediaeval philosophy. The difficulty," he continued, "is our people; our solicitors that is: they say Somerset could cause a bit of damage; you know, make a case, as it were. We've offered to assist with some shifting costs and all of that ... I mean, damn it, there's plenty of other universities his daughter could carry on with your mediaeval guff but bloody Somerset has the bit between his teeth and ... anyway ... to cut things short we have a proposal to put to you."

"Oh yes," Professor Trout said, intuitively sensing that at long last revenge was nigh. "What are you suggesting?"

"Well," the Vice-Chancellor said, eying the professor carefully. "What we ... that is, the University Council were wondering ... what we thought would sort things out tidily and leave everyone happy – all resolved if you follow me – was if you could see your way clear to neatly wrap everything up, think a little outside the square as it were, and award your uncompleted students their degrees here and now – just to put a cap on things, if you follow me."

"No."

"No?"

"Yes: no!"

"Come now, Professor Trout. Let us not be overly precious. No disrespect intended, but why on earth does it matter? I mean, let's be sensible: it's hardly life and death. It's not as if I'm asking you to pass someone doing something that counts

– you know, an electrician or motor mechanic or what have you. Goodness me, let's be realistic. It's mediaeval philosophy, dammit! Who cares? Why does it matter?"

"I care, and I have no doubt so do my students; and it does matter – very much, in fact."

The Vice-Chancellor's face darkened. "I see. Well, I'd rather hoped you might be more co-operative. Think about the wider picture ... the greater good for the university and all of that. After all, Professor, you've enjoyed a lifetime here at Ralston and one might reasonably ..."

"No," Professor Trout said firmly. "That, Vice-Chancellor, is my absolute answer."

There was an awkward lull.

Eventually Professor Trout broke the impasse. "If that's everything, then if you'll forgive me, I have work to do," and leaving the Vice-Chancellor sullenly brooding he rose and left.

CHAPTER EIGHTEEN

"**Y**OU ARE CONFRONTED by a universal problem, Mr Thomas, and certainly have my sympathy," Professor Trout said gently to the anxious postgraduate student sitting opposite. "Finding a thesis topic in the traditional disciplines not already done to death is a dilemma facing doctoral aspirants everywhere. While Fulbert's school of Chartres was certainly momentous, simply describing it as you propose is insufficient as a thesis subject."

Noting his student's crestfallen demeanour, Professor Trout continued. "What you require is an angle: a fresh approach – that, after all, is the whole point of scholarship."

"But what?" Thomas cried. "You've often complimented me on my knowledge of the Chartres school. I assure you, Professor, I've read every word on the subject – well, in English, that is. You can hardly expect me to learn German and French just to access their material," he laughed.

"You're rather missing the point, Mr Thomas. Even should you uncover new material not previously published in English – which I suspect would be highly unlikely – that in itself would not constitute scholarship. Regardless of language, the information would already be on the table and your role would be mere reportage."

"But I can scarcely make things up," the student protested.

"Nor should you," Professor Trout replied. "That most certainly would not be scholarship." He paused and thought for a few moments. "The whole point of academic scholarship is first to acquire all of the known information and then to draw conclusions; to try to establish patterns, to speculate as to causes and effects and ponder on the elements of chance and how things might have eventuated differently, had perhaps someone not got out of bed on the wrong side one morning, for example. Simply re-presenting existing knowledge is unhelpful. We are not here to merely conserve information."

"I'd have thought that's exactly what we do, Professor; you know: conserve historic knowledge."

The Professor's face clouded. "If I thought that, Mr Thomas, then I would consider my professional life to have been wasted. Think about it. Conservatives in any form – political, religious fundamentalists or in the environmental sphere – are all unwitting enemies of scholarship and human progress. Their desire to conserve reflects their closed minds, lacking imagination, blind to the ever-changing and evolving nature of life and demonstrably ignorant in their certainties.

Your acquired knowledge of mediaeval philosophy does not constitute an end in itself but is instead rich material to apply creatively."

"It seems damned unfair, Professor. A friend of mine is doing his sociology doctorate on why Bradford factory workers go to pubs after work. It's dead easy. He's just handing out questionnaires with a range of tick-the-box categories, then he's feeding it all into his computer to collate. There's none of this speculation and scholarship stuff."

Professor Trout hesitated, his mind awash with different responses. As a personal practice he was reluctant to criticize another discipline unless it was in the absurd Rubenesque Studies category. Sociology, if a valid information-recording activity, was hardly intellectually rigorous, and academically unworthy of university study, let alone doctoral status. In the Professor's view it was not as socially useful as, say, plumbing or nursing, but he would concede it a minor function, belonging at best in the polytechnics as essentially a data-collection process about group behaviour which too often simply stated the obvious.

"You have chosen to study mediaeval philosophy," he said eventually. "In itself it has no direct application to contemporary life. Rather, it is a foundation for intellectual development; for acquiring perspective and for honing your imagination and sharpening your mind, all wonderful tools for whatever future lies ahead of you. In that context, as I have said, the speculative element becomes all-important; not the mere acquisition of a set of facts."

"My speculations might be nonsense," Thomas muttered sulkily.

"Yes indeed," Professor Trout replied. "But if they're feasible conclusions, well founded in logic, regardless of whether they're right or wrong they contribute to our field, and additionally, assist future students in stretching their mental horizons beyond simply learning elementary factual matter." His tone became brisk. "Now I suggest if you apply your thinking along those lines you will be surprised how the problem you perceive is less of a hurdle than it seems. Let me give you an example of what you could consider. As you know, Fulbert opened the school of Chartres in 990, yet it was not until the twelfth century that it received recognition as Europe's most illustrious centre of learning. There indeed is a topic worthy of a doctorate, namely: why did it take a century and more to flower? Part of the answer is obvious: namely the slowness of communications in those times. But what other factors possibly applied? Was there resistance to Fulbert's thinking? Were other centres and accepted prevailing thought so dominant that it took time to override them? Was the school poorly run in the years after Fulbert's death? We know that under Bernard's stewardship, for five years early in the twelfth century the Chartres school reached its zenith – so what of those intervening years? I suggest you weigh what I have said and return tomorrow and I am sure we can reach a satisfactory outcome."

Scarcely had Thomas gone when there was a knock on the door. The Vice-Chancellor's secretary, Miss Hampton, entered, ushering before her a plainly shy, pretty young

Oriental woman wearing a colourful sarong and decorative blouse, which costume the Professor wrongly assumed was Thai or Burmese.

"Spare a minute, Professor?" Miss Hampton asked, and without waiting for an answer, "This is Miss Phomsouvanh. She's from Laos. Unfortunately she doesn't speak English."

The girl lifted her head briefly and clasped her two hands together in greeting, then resumed her study of the floor.

"I'm just showing her around," Miss Hampton explained. "She starts with your department tomorrow as one of our 168 new scholarship recipients brought in on Ralston's multi-nation student strategy."

"But if she doesn't speak English she can't possibly join us," Professor Trout protested.

Miss Hampton shifted awkwardly. "You will have to take that up with the Vice-Chancellor, Professor. I'm just following orders," and she quickly ushered Miss Phomsouvanh from the room.

Professor Trout did indeed take it up with the Vice-Chancellor – ten minutes later, once again bursting in un-announced.

"I invite you to take a broader view of the matter, Professor," the Vice-Chancellor said testily. "The scholarship scheme is a new concept and we must anticipate these initial teething difficulties."

"But if she doesn't speak English what on earth is the point? Has she a philosophy background in Laos?"

The Vice-Chancellor examined a thick binder containing

the scholarship students' background information, then laughed dryly. "Seemingly not. I'm afraid she's from a village in northern Laos, near the Vietnamese border. I'm not sure if she's even been to school, but that's not the point. Miss Phomsouvanh will receive a holiday in England which may be her only opportunity to ever leave her village: and in return we will receive the benefit of her presence vis-à-vis the underlying objective of the scholarship programme, namely an enrolment-building publicity device."

"This is preposterous!" Professor Trout exclaimed. "For God's sake, why waste the opportunity? Why not give the scholarships to genuine students?"

"I admire your idealism, Professor. Unfortunately – and, I might say, unsurprisingly – you have overlooked the practical elements. As you know, this scheme is essentially targeting impoverished third-world countries. Naturally we did as you suggested and placed such a prescription on our scholarships. But sadly, in those sorts of places life is not like that. They're all riddled with corruption and it would appear our scholarships have been sold by the education authorities in each country to the highest bidder. Miss Phomsouvanh's father is reputedly a highly successful smuggler across the Vietnamese border and he was concerned about his daughter forming what he viewed as an unsuitable attachment. Purchasing our scholarship provided him with an excellent opportunity to eliminate his problem. I am quite sure you will find Miss Phomsouvanh no trouble, Professor. She will attend your classes assiduously – although obviously not in any participation sense."

"Then surely she would be better off in one of your nonsense activities," the Professor spluttered. "Line-dancing or witchcraft or whatever."

The Vice-Chancellor bristled at the word "nonsense". "I hardly need you to point that out, Professor Cod, but once again you overlook the practical elements. It is those fields of scholarship which are already bulging at the seams, while your department on the other hand has considerable capacity for more pupils. Aside from that, your derisory view of those activities is not borne out by the evidence. We have, where opportunity allows, done exactly as you suggest, but I'm afraid you rather over-estimate the abilities of these foreign scholars."

"What do you mean?" the Professor asked.

"For example, last week our two New Guinea scholarship students arrived and we placed them in the panelbeating department. Apparently they were sons of a hill-tribe chief who'd delivered his village's votes to the Education Minister and in turn was repaid with the scholarships. Unfortunately they nearly burned the building down with blow-torches on their first day, Professor Whale. No: all things considered it is far better you pitch in and co-operate. Miss Phomsouvanh can do no harm in your department. Just pay her no attention."

"This is unadulterated madness!" Professor Trout exploded.

The Vice-Chancellor stiffened. "I am deeply disappointed in your inability to adopt a more co-operative attitude, Professor Crabb. In the broad sweep of things, the issues you raise are of no moment. It is a great pity that you cannot take a leaf from Mr Frewen's book. He has been typically co-operative and has willingly taken the two New Guinea scholars under his wing in the Rubenesque Studies department, notwithstanding space there being at a premium. He is an academic who commendably embraces the new Ralston spirit going forward."

So Miss Phomsouvanh joined the mediaeval philosophy department and, as the Vice-Chancellor predicted, she proved trouble-free, sitting expressionless in the lecture-room as debate on St Thomas Aquinas, Isadore of Seville, Lanfranc and Augustinianism flowed about her.

In the event she was to provide final testimony of Professor Trout's inability to comprehend the modern world when looking out of his barracks window one afternoon he observed Thomas, now embarked on his thesis topic, "Factors in Delayed Acceptance of Fulbert's Doctrine", sitting hand-in-hand with Miss Phomsouvanh. Plainly language difficulties were not of consequence to the modern generation in the new order.

CHAPTER NINETEEN

"WELL?" PROFESSOR TROUT enquired expectantly when Frewen arrived on Tuesday; and when there was no immediate response, "Come now Mr Frewen, tell me: how did it all go?" Then, observing Frewen's downcast expression, "Oh dear – problems?"

"The poo again," Frewen muttered dolefully, plonking himself heavily in a seat.

"Goodness! I'm certainly sorry to hear that. I can assure you I put quite some effort into your address so I'm as disappointed as …"

"No, no. Wasn't the speech; least not in the sense of it not going down well. Far from it. Just the opposite in fact. That was the damned problem."

"I'm sorry; I don't understand."

"Don't suppose you heard about me getting arrested?" Frewen mumbled.

"Of course I did. It was in all of the newspapers."

"That right!" Frewen remarked, plainly surprised. "Well fancy that."

"But surely you must have seen them," Professor Trout queried. "You were on the front page of the *Guardian*, and with a photo of you, and also in the *Telegraph*, and I imagine the others."

"Thing is, Prof, newspapers have never really been my forté. Price of a busy life, I suppose. Still ..."

"But you were a ..." Professor Trout began, then thought better of it. "Never mind. Tell me what happened."

"Bloody embarrassing, I can tell you," Frewen grumbled. "Still, with the career on the line as it were – bloody Beefy gave me that message loud and clear – I did what she told me and knocked a policeman's helmet off. Felt a damn fool, believe me. Anyway, they threw me in the slammer; damned rude about it too – I see no call for that – and then there was the court the next day. Got fined a hundred quid, but when I came out all the fat girls were waiting and cheering and Beefy told me I was a hero but to say nothing to the press – she handled all of that – and she even paid the fine so that was alright. Then we went off to Clone ..." he paused ... "I say, Prof, did you know they don't speak English there?"

"Yes. That's not entirely surprising. They're Germans, you see."

Frewen pondered this. "Still, be that as it may ... you'd think ..."

"Did you enjoy Cologne?" the Professor interrupted.

"Bloody meal services were slow, I can tell you," Frewen said. "The hotel was packed with the conference delegates."

Professor Trout briefly puzzled over this response, then: "Are you telling me you never actually looked around the city?"

This time it was Frewen's turn for bewilderment. "Looked around at what, Prof?"

Professor Trout decided to abandon this line of enquiry. "What happened at the conference?" he asked, now on tenterhooks as to the cause of Frewen's fresh troubles.

"Well, we kicked off on the Saturday and Beefy and I were first off the block after the opening stuff. Three hundred women from all over the world – and a handful of bearded blokes too," he added, fingering his own unruly beard. "Little wimpy blokes, they all were. Mind you, I can't say there were any a chap would fancy: the females that is. Lotsa fat ones, and between you and me, Professor, they were mostly pretty damned peculiar; not your normal run of women, if you get my drift. Funny thing was, most of them looked like blokes actually. Anyway, Beefy got up and read her speech, then she introduced me and went on and on about the protest and my arrest and all of that carry-on and then all those weird fat women stood up and shouted and clapped me for about five minutes. Tell you what, though. Got rid of my nerves, all that cheering for me. Never had that before. Anyway, I read the damned speech, or tried to – some of those big words were a bit tricky – and when I was finished they all got up and started cheering again; and it more or less confirmed what

I'd felt all along, you know, about finding my true vocation as an academic. Not that I ever expected to be famous, mind. That was a surprise."

"I'm afraid you have me at a loss, Mr Frewen," the Professor said. "It sounds like a huge success – hardly the poo as you suggested."

Frewen shuffled awkwardly. "That was the bloody problem. Scored an own-goal, basically. The old Beefenstein hung on to me like a limpet all that day; sort of showing me off and praising me all the time. I even signed autographs. Never done that before, either. Then that night there was a conference dinner. I should have guessed what was to come when old Beefy started holding my hand under the table, so at the first opportunity I snuck off to bed.

"Anyway, there I was lying in the dark minding my business when my door opened and there in the half-light looming up was Beefy in a white nightie like a bloody great portable tent. It was a terrifying sight for a chap I can tell you. After that … well I know I've put on a fair bit lately but with bloody Beefy, I was way out of my weight class. Didn't stand a chance. There was no stopping her, Prof. I don't wish to sound ungrateful but I reckon it was a bit of a blunder banging that bit in my speech about my great admiration for her. Got her wound up, if you get my drift."

"I see," Professor Trout said flatly.

"Mind you, what actually occurred I can't really be absolutely sure," Frewen hurried on. "I mean I was sort of engulfed and I just assume everything happened in the right place, if you get my drift. But it was impossible to tell, with all those great rolls of fat and …"

"I don't wish to know those details," the Professor interrupted tersely; then, more encouragingly, "This sort of thing is not uncommon at conferences, so I'm told."

"That's not the point!" Frewen spluttered. "Eventually she buggered off and the next morning when I was in the breakfast room hoeing in, in she came, spotted me and sort of skipped over, almost like she was dancing – a fearful sight, Professor, with someone her size, believe me. She was all over me like a rash, then she announced I was promoted to a senior lecturer, which of course was bloody good news salary-wise."

"You have my congratulations, Mr Frewen. So why the distress?"

"After she told me she'd been on the phone to the Vice-Chancellor and he'd agreed that I'd be promoted …" he paused and gazed crestfallen at Professor Trout.

"Yes. Go on. What's the problem?"

"She more or less insisted that I had to be on duty as it were, at least two nights a week at her flat if you get my drift, and hinted pretty damn clearly, make no mistake, that if I wasn't in it then I was out."

"Quite a dilemma, Mr Frewen," the Professor said, concealing his delight with some difficulty.

"Bloody dilemma all right – be a bloody miracle more like if I can manage it. I'm barely coping on the home front as it is. And then, to top all that, today she's come up with another damned brainwave. She's hired a Japanese bloke and three mornings a week all the fat girls and I have to learn bloody sumo wrestling. The thing is, sport's never really been my strong point you see. Not my forté at all. She says sumo is the only true sport and I have to master it. Never actually told you this, Prof, but it's my left leg, you see," he added mysteriously. "Had it all my life."

"What? A left leg?"

"'Fraid so. Doctors amazed, they are," and he shook his head solemnly. "So you can see why bloody sumo's a problem. All this stuff is a side of the scholar's life I just never anticipated." He stopped and mulled it all over, then, "Mind you, I suppose you had to do the same to become a professor?"

"No, Mr Frewen, I can safely say we philosophers feel no need to indulge in sumo wrestling."

"I didn't mean that, dammit! I mean joisting on horseback and all that mediaeval carrying-on. Did all that, did you?"

"We maintain a detachment, I'm afraid," Professor Trout responded gravely. "Perhaps you will condemn us for failing to adopt a more hands-on, practical approach to our field of scholarship. If so, then I can assure you it is a viewpoint the Vice-Chancellor would unhesitatingly endorse."

Frewen pondered this information. Suddenly he brightened. "I say, Prof, that's the answer. I should switch over to your line. Solve the Beefy and sumo problems in one go! Do you reckon you could squeeze me in – not as a professor to start with, of course. Appreciate you've got that wrapped up; and anyway, I'd have to get the hang of your stuff first; but, say, kicking off as a lecturer, or if you could see your way clear, given my promotion, as a senior lecturer."

"That sounds a first-rate proposal," the Professor replied, struggling to maintain a straight face. "We'd certainly appreciate having you. Unfortunately, far from employing new staff, the Vice-Chancellor is intent on actually reducing our teaching personnel … so under the circumstances, regrettably, we will have to forgo this opportunity."

"Mmm … I could have a chat with the Vice-Chancellor. He was damn decent over the panelbeating adjustment and obviously didn't want to lose me. And come to think of it, he owes me. He came over two weeks ago and delivered a couple of darkies. Said he was relying on me to look after them; take them under my wing as it were. Part of some new deal he's running bringing in wogs from everywhere. Funny buggers, they are. Never say a peep. They cart Bibles about and have their noses in them all the time. Last thing we need are bloody Bible-bashers. They're from a place called New Guinea; in Africa I think. You heard of it, Professor?"

"Yes. But not quite Africa I'm afraid: a different ethnic group altogether."

"Is that so? Oh well, ethnics never really were my forté. Don't know about you Prof, but darkies all look the same to me. Anyway, like I said I reckon it could be worth me having a word with the Vice-Chancellor: after all, I've kept an eye on the savages like he asked. Strange, though: I'm not sure they're learning much. They haven't written any essays, but the Vice-Chancellor says we've got to pass them anyway. They just sit there eyeing the fat girls – and they get really excited when old Beefy comes in."

"Perhaps they could take your, ah, servicing obligations to your professor off your hands," Professor Trout suggested mischievously.

Frewen shot up erect from his normal slumping posture. "I say, Prof! That's a brilliant idea. Do you reckon she'd go for it?"

"I boast no expertise in these matters, Mr Frewen. However, I imagine with a little constructive input from your good self in facilitating the appropriate circumstances, given, as you say, your professor's intensity on the one hand and the two students' beguilement with her on the other, one might reasonably allow at least the possibility of a satisfactory culmination, all things being equal."

Frewen looked puzzled. "Don't quite get your drift, Prof. You sound just like the Vice-Chancellor. Whatta you reckon I should do?"

Irked at the comparison with his bête noire, Professor Trout struggled with this unfamiliar poser. "It's not the type of conundrum I'm accustomed to dealing with, Mr Frewen. Nevertheless, I don't imagine there have been significant procedural changes in courtship practices since I was a youth. I presume the standard strategies still apply: of dining together and going out to …"

"That's it, by God!" Frewen exclaimed excitedly. "Dining – just what the bloody doctor ordered! There's no keener knife-and-fork exponent than the old Beefenstein. But hang on ..." and his face creased in concentration as he struggled with a fresh dilemma. "Snag I see is: how do we get old Beefy to be in it?"

"Really, Mr Frewen! I would have thought the solution to that was obvious. You could act as an intermediary and suggest to the two students ... no, under the circumstances of the task in hand, perhaps you could go a trifle further and not merely suggest but instruct them, that convention requires them to host their professor in their dormitory.

"Then you simply tell the Professor that the two gentlemen concerned much admire her, but being a little shy they have consulted you, and that they wish to host her to a traditional New Guinean banquet. After that, and having established fixtures, one must simply trust nature to take its course – and as always with such speculative scenarios, pray for a little luck."

"You're a bloody genius, Prof!" Frewen cried ecstatically. "I'll get stuck in smartly – get the ball rolling, as it were."

"Why thank you, Mr Frewen. I assume such matters are as you sometimes put it, not your forté, and as always I'm happy to assist where I can. I shall look forward with interest to your reports on progress in the endeavour."

Frewen's face screwed up. "Problem I see is, if they're bloody Bible-bashers, they probably won't be in the necessary stuff. I don't think the old Beefenstein's looking for a damned prayer meeting."

"There, indeed, I can offer some advice," Professor Trout said. "It has been my life-long observation that the more fervent is Christian advocacy, the more inclined its promulgators are, when it suits them, to ignore its essential moral tenets. It is admittedly a field for the behavioural disciplines, but nevertheless I have observed that extremism in any form tends to display a polarizing propensity when circumstances change."

"Don't quite get your drift, Prof. Are you saying I should have a crack at it?"

"That, indeed, is my position on the matter, Mr Frewen – although I qualify it by conceding it is merely an opinion."

Later that evening Professor Trout reflected on this exchange, slightly uneasy at how deeply he was becoming enmeshed in Frewen's affairs. Frewen had passed beyond a hobby to verging on an obsession.

No matter, he ultimately concluded. Very soon he would be at St Andrews, where Frewenism would be non-existent. It had certainly enlivened his otherwise black last two years to entertain himself in this manner; and in any event it was all perfectly harmless. Ultimately nature would or would not take its course and either outcome could be of no consequence.

CHAPTER TWENTY

"Ah," Professor Trout sighed contentedly. At last some deeper thinking. He was marking his second-year students' essays and had already scored the first five with Cs and added critical handwritten comments.

The topic, "Can a philosopher without philosophy still be a philosopher? Comment in the context of Bonaventure", had been set in the hope of generating some lively argument, but so far only Angela Somerset appeared to have taken up the challenge when she wrote:

> At face value Bonaventure was not a philosopher.
>
> The essence of his thinking can be encapsulated in the preface to the second volume of his main work, "Commentary on the Sentences" when he wrote: "Just as in the first book I adhered to the general judgements and opinions of the masters ... so in the following book I shall not turn back from their path.

I do not, moreover, wish to combat new opinions, but to develop old ones." In short, Bonaventure relied entirely on accepted doctrine to merely reinforce existing values. When he wrote, "The order is to begin from the stability of faith through the serenity of reason to contemplation," at a philosophical level, he effectively disqualified himself from consideration as a philosopher and instead, in his role as the Franciscan Chair appointed by the Pope, clearly felt dutybound to propagate church teaching in the guise of philosophic scholarship.

But that is only on face value, for despite the rigidity of his approach in confining his thinking within the boundaries of Christian doctrine, when viewed in the context of prevailing thirteenth-century thought, a case can be argued to categorize him as a philosopher. To begin with there is the semantic aspect as to what is a philosopher?

For example, in an age when readership was largely confined to religious tomes which were always read aloud, suggesting ritual rather than thought in the exercise, one can ask whether a philosopher need necessarily present new ideas, which Bonaventure certainly did not.

But nor did Adam Smith five centuries later. Every Smith proposition was derivative so, despite his academic background in philosophy and his later role as the Chair of Moral Philosophy at Glasgow

University, his strengths lay in putting the already-known pieces of his personal jigsaw together, and also in their readable presentation. But no-one questions his philosophic credentials because …

A knock on the door disturbed Professor Trout just as he was reaching the interesting part. He looked up, annoyed at the disturbance, as the door opened and a beaming Vice-Chancellor entered, followed by a small olive-complexioned, ferret-faced man wearing a garish double-breasted, grey and red pin-striped suit with a flamboyant posy pinned to his lapel. A luxuriant and obvious toupee sat above a face of indescribable evil. Behind him followed two hulking thugs wearing dark glasses.

"Professor Trout!" the Vice-Chancellor exclaimed. "So pleased to find you in. Allow me to introduce Mr Vassillo." The two brutes hovered stolidly by the door and were ignored.

Vassillo darted forward, his hand extended. "Moik's the nime; entertoinment's the gime," he exclaimed. "Noice to meet ya Prof," as the startled Professor Trout rose and shook hands.

"Mr Vassillo is a very successful businessman," the Vice-Chancellor gushed. "He has graciously agreed to sponsor the Mediaeval Philosophy Department, and in acknowledgement I'm pleased to inform you that this fine building is to become the Vassillo Philosophy Hall from next month."

"Loik oi said, entertoinment's the gime," Vassillo enthused. "Moybe not your cup a toi you'll be thinking Prof but we get all sorts – cabinet ministers, bishops, ambassadors, company directors – you name it, we see 'em all. Ever ya down in London oi'll see ya roight. Show ya a good time in our VIP room, know wot oi mean?" and he reached in his pocket then handed Professor Trout a business card.

It bore a Soho address and read,

Michael Vassillo

Proprietor

Exotique Nightclub

50 international beautiful ladies at your service

This information was enclosed in an illustration of a crest being held aloft by two leering naked girls. A crown sat atop the crest.

"Oi got six other 'stablishments," Vassillo boasted. "Oi'm in Manchester, Leeds, Birmingham, Liverpool, Nottingham and Sheffield and oi'm building new premises in Brighton. Opening next momf. Get where the action is; know what oi mean Prof?"

"Mr Vassillo is taken with the concept of association with a philosophy department," the Vice-Chancellor proffered.

"Yeah. If me ol' mum back in Malta could see me now," Vassillo said dreamily. "The Vassillo Phlosophy Hall: she'd be roight proud." He screwed up his face grotesquely to indicate a forthcoming solemn utterance, "See, the fing you don't understand, Prof, is me mum's actually Greek" – this said as if Professor Trout had been contesting the matter – "it's me Dad's that's Maltese, so you'll be understanding about phlosophy bein' in me blood – on me mum's side, loik."

The Vice-Chancellor leapt in to fill the void which followed this utterance.

"Yes indeed, Mr Vassillo. A great tradition. You should be very proud."

"I think the Vice-Chancellor is referring to your cultural heritage," Professor Trout said dryly. The Vice-Chancellor shot him a glare but the undercurrent between them was lost on Vassillo.

"Quite roight Professor. Once it's in the blood you can't 'elp yourself, know what oi mean? Always been phlosophic about fings, oi 'ave meself. In moi profession fings go wrong efry day. Can't run a stable wif two hundred ladies wifout serious trouble big time. You know what women are loik Prof: take a liberty quick as look at ya. 'Ave to be phlosophic, oi do. Me and you are in the same gime Professor. Bofe phlosophers we are."

"Once the signage is up we'll be sending you a large framed photograph of the building and also a framed certificate of commemoration from the university to hang alongside it," the Vice-Chancellor said unctuously. "Now if you'll excuse us, Professor Trout, I'll take Mr Vassillo back to my office for afternoon tea."

Later that day he returned. "Not quite the sort of prestige brand business we had in mind but it's a start," he ventured. "We have a chap, Max Bradford, full-time on the road selling our Chairs and buildings naming rights. He's a client of Mr Vassillo, so he had the inside running. I gather Bradford is an expert exponent of one of the new fashionable dance recreations – something called lap-dancing, which apparently Mr Vassillo's establishments specialise in. Different from our day, what, Professor? Then it was all waltzes and the quick-step. Still, I pride myself on the university's modernity and I'll have my people look into it. The line-dancing school has certainly been a splendid success and if the interest is there we will affiliate a lap-dancing department to it. Doubtless Bradford will be well placed to become our first lap-dancing professor – assuming of course that he does indeed know all the moves. Fundraising is never a cakewalk but Bradford has about a dozen balls in the air so far and some of those will land. Early days yet.

"Vassillo's paying £50,000 for five years' naming rights to this building. He turned up in a yellow Rolls-Royce so I tried to persuade him to endow a Chair; even offered him an honorary doctorate and I could see he was taken with the idea but I suspect half a million for the Chair of Philosophy naming rights may have been a little out of his league. Still, like I said, it's a start in the right direction. Handled right, I don't doubt in due course he might be disposed to part with £100,000 for an honorary doctorate. Naturally they're not something we should issue lightly. Don't want to devalue the Ralston name but £100,000 seems fair to all parties, all things considered. One innovation I'm considering is issuing our own Ralston Distinguished Service to Education medals. Say £10,000 a pop – annual black-tie presentation dinner function, guest speaker, you know, the type of thing businessmen like. There's certainly a market there going untapped. Anyway, I imagine you're happy about it. To be candid, I never anticipated there would be any interest in sponsorship with the humanities departments; but if this keeps up, then consideration will have to be given to retaining some of them."

"Fortunately I shall not be here to witness any of that," Professor Trout said tersely.

"Yes indeed; which brings me to the point of my visit," the Vice-Chancellor said. "Vassillo's rather excited by all of this. He mentioned his intention of returning to show his friends his name on the building. I could hardly deter him, so should he do so I would be grateful if you would treat him with courtesy; indeed all things considered it would be helpful if you were to act a little deferentially, especially should he have his associates with him. It's not too much to ask in your last few weeks."

"You mean afternoon tea; or should I offer him a sherry?" the Professor responded scathingly.

"I don't see either option as a hardship," the Vice-Chancellor said curtly. "But that aside, the principal purpose of my visit is to request that you exercise appropriate prudence should he return. I'm referring to next door – you know, the School of Paedophiliac Studies. It's part of this building and there's always the possibility Vassillo might not take kindly to association with the more modern disciplines. If he's running ballroom establishments then he's bound to be excessively concerned about matters of decorum and probably possesses old-fashioned and somewhat prudish views, particularly given his Latin background. Not a man of the world like you and me, Professor. That probably surprises you, but I have considerable experience in dealing with businessmen and as a general proposition I think it's fair to say they tend towards a highly conservative and somewhat moralistic outlook and do not have the same liberal approach to these matters that you or I do."

"If he does turn up then he can scarcely fail to see all the perverts skulking about," the Professor observed cuttingly.

"Please refer to them as scholars," the Vice-Chancellor snapped. "Should he encounter them then I have no doubt he will assume they're philosophers – more so, as most look the part."

"Oh? And how is that?" the Professor asked, taken aback.

"Middle-aged males, somewhat pensive, mind on other matters – seemingly away with the fairies – it's a commonality in demeanour with you philosophy types I observed right from the outset of the opening of the Paedophiliac Studies School," the Vice-Chancellor replied. "I merely remind you that in such an event there is no need for elucidation." He turned and walked to the door, then stopped. "Oh, there's one other matter, Professor. You're leaving us shortly. I thought perhaps a small farewell function; two or perhaps at a stretch three of your closer colleagues; and possibly you may have a senior student you …"

"That won't be necessary, thank you," Professor Trout cut in. In fact he had already arranged to host such a gathering on his final day, now only a fortnight away.

CHAPTER TWENTY-ONE

HE LAST DAY OF Professor Trout's career at Ralston fell on a Monday, but it did not occur to him to stay at home. The previous week he had removed his personal effects and apart from his desk, some chairs and a marble bust of Plato, all items belonging to the university, his study was now empty.

On Monday morning he loaded his car with two crates of wine and a box of wine glasses. Enid was bringing canapés at 3.30pm, when the sixteen academic colleagues and eight senior students he had invited would arrive for his farewell drinks party. It was only while driving to the university that it crossed his mind he would have nothing to do until his guests arrived.

The Professor parked his car, intending to telephone for a porter to bring the crates across later. As he had done for four decades, he set out through the portals of the ancient stone building and into the spacious quad, its cobblestone surface worn smooth over the past two centuries. He felt no nostalgia, only relief at his departure.

"Morning Geoffrey," he greeted the wizened head porter Cone, who was reaching into a crate delivered each Monday morning containing ten justifiably anxious chickens required for the Religious Studies Department's popular Applied Voodooism diploma course. Cone delivered two chickens to the voodooists each morning for ceremonial sacrificial purposes, before setting out on his bent-double ritual morning shuffle across the quad to unlock its centrepiece chapel.

For two centuries the chapel had remained permanently open, but following complaints from Muslim students the Education Office had banned Christian services and it was now used as a lecture theatre. The McNally suicide had necessitated that the porter check each morning that no-one else had similarly lost heart and followed the Irishman's example.

"Arghh ... morn-eg 'fessor, arghh ..." Cone mumbled, slowly straightening as he withdrew that day's victims.

To the thump, thump, thump background racket of trashy pop music, a recent innovation now piped throughout the university, Professor Trout reached the chapel which, having survived the Vice-Chancellor's failed attempt to lift its Heritage Trust listing and replace it with a high-rise building, was now the home of the line-dancing department.

Along its reaches, on the antique oak pews which had been removed from inside and were now painted green, sprawled the bovine lady line-dancing scholars, gazing vacuously as they awaited Cone's arrival. Shapeless and heavy-legged, all were clad in peasant-style skirts with dark-glasses-topped stetsons on their heads. Professor Trout studied with distaste their blank, porridgy, porcine-eyed faces and tiny, pursed, scarlet-painted mouths.

He passed the locked chapel doors where the male line-dancing scholars, also stetson-hatted, lingered. They, by contrast, were all unhealthily desiccated; many had pencil moustaches and all wore tasselled leather jackets, cowboy boots and string ties overlaid with several gold chains from which dangled a range of banal metal ornamental objects. Some wore toy six-shooters on their hips and one had a lasso lying in coils across his shoulder. Their faces were gaunt and chinless and they slouched in small silent groups cupping roll-your-own cigarettes. Collectively, they bore an air of criminal depravity and Professor Trout shuddered at the thought of their graduation ceremony, seeing them gowned and with dark glasses atop their mortar boards.

Averting his eyes from this depressing spectacle, for the last time Professor Trout looked across to Anselm Hall in the far corner of the quad, his domain until two years earlier, but his attention was seized by an outburst of loud chanting. Up ahead he observed a hundred black-robed applied witchcraft students sitting cross-legged in a large circle, eyes closed, rhythmically raising and lowering their arms to their chanting. Cavorting wild-eyed in their midst and holding a goat on a leash while waving an animal bone with his other hand, was the former nuclear physics lecturer, now the Professor of Applied Witchcraft.

Professor Trout picked his way round the witchcraft scholars who, unlike the line dancers, were adorned with flesh-piercing metal rings. He reached Chaucer Hall, home for two centuries of Ralston's much-vaunted classics library, now in storage awaiting despatch to America, and was instantly assailed by the powerful aroma of frying beef and onions. For Chaucer Hall was now the abode of the burgeoning new Hamburgerology Department, and would soon be ceremoniously renamed McDonalds Hall, the Vice-Chancellor having secured £1 million for naming rights to the building.

Rounding the corner, the Professor abruptly found himself confronted by eight police cars, an ambulance and numerous loitering policemen preoccupied in the consumption of hamburgers supplied through the open windows of the Hamburgerology Department.

A policeman, clipboard in one hand and a hamburger in the other, stepped forward. "'Scuse me, Sir. Only authorised personnel allowed any further," he said.

Professor Trout identified himself and the officer placed his hamburger on a police-car roof and flicked through his notes. "Just made it, Sir. The cut-off point is Building J. Please stay in your premises. You'll find yellow tape dividing the no-go zone. In no circumstances cross to the other side."

Realizing his assumption that a raid on the Paedophilia Department was clearly wrong if his building was not out of bounds, Professor Trout enquired what was happening.

"Sorry, Sir. Not at liberty to comment. You'll find out soon enough," and the policeman turned away and resumed his hamburger consumption.

Entering his study, Professor Trout was relieved to find Frewen slouched in a seat, finishing off a hamburger. Not only would he know what the trouble was, but the prospect of an hour or so's Frewenist badinage appealed, not just in filling the time, for the Professor felt an unexpected ambivalence at the thought of no more Frewenism in his life. The morning's mail and a small package lay on his desk. He would open them later. "Good morning, Mr Frewen," he said in a more welcoming tone than usual.

"Thank God you've come, Prof. I need your advice urgently!" Frewen cried, as he swallowed the last hamburger remnant and wiped his hands on his corduroy trousers.

"What's going on with all those policemen? Have you any idea?"

"Oh, them: that's just bloody Beefy and the savages," Frewen said nonchalantly. "Surprised you don't know about that, Prof."

"Why? What's happened?" Professor Trout demanded.

"I set everything up like you said for last Tuesday night. When I told Beefy about the ..." he hesitated, "Where's it again? You know: the wog place the two darkies I told you about come from."

"New Guinea."

"Yeah; that's it. Well, I put the hard word on those New Guinea blokes like you said. Turned out they could speak English – sort of, anyway – so that wasn't a problem. I told them to slap on a traditional wog banquet and then, like you said, I let old Beefy know they were expecting her. She was over the moon. Not sure if it was the darkies or the food she was most excited about, but I was keeping my fingers crossed it was the savages.

"Anyway, on Friday it occurred to me I hadn't seen her for a few days – not that I wanted to, specially since the conference. Then, yesterday afternoon the Vice-Chancellor rang and made me come in – said there was crisis – a bit bloody rich when you think about it, Prof: having to work on a Sunday and not getting extra pay."

"Yes, yes, but what happened?" Professor Trout demanded with a sinking sense of pending disaster.

"When I drove up there were bloody coppers everywhere and then a black bloke arrived in a chauffeured car with a flag on it. Turned out he was the New Guinean High Commissioner. Apparently that's like an ambassador, Prof. Anyway, he went off with the coppers and the Vice-Chancellor to talk to the New Guinea students ..." Frewen paused, his mind plainly on other matters. "You know, Prof, we academics should start a union; establish working hours and get overtime if we have to ..."

"For God's sake, Frewen, get to the point! What's happened?"

"They've eaten her! Scoffed the lot!"

"Who? What do you mean? Who's eaten whom?"

"Well, not the lot, I s'pose. Couldn't manage that in four days. I mean, even after they'd gutted her I reckon there'd have to be three hundred pounds of meat left. Lotta fat, of course, with old Beefy, but they may have kept some of the innards. Don't know about you, Prof, but personally I'm not averse to a nice bit of fried liver and a kidney or two. Anyway, they'd knocked off one leg and a bit of rump steak and they were having the rest as cold cuts and getting through her pretty damn quick. Seems they'd invited some of those other special scholarship wog students over to help out. Blokes from a place called the Solomon Islands and another outfit called Vanua or Vanuati or something like that. The Vice-Chancellor said they all speak the same lingo."

"Frewen!" the Professor shouted. "Stop being so oblique! What exactly has happened?"

"I told you," Frewen said tetchily. "They cooked old Beefy and ate her. Well, like I said, not all of her, but with those Solomon and Vanu-something blokes on the job as well, they were ready to start on the other leg. Would have, too, if the cleaners hadn't found her stashed under one of their beds."

After a lengthy pause the Professor asked in a quavering voice, "Are you absolutely certain?"

"Of course I am. The Vice-Chancellor told me all about it. According to the High Commission joker, back home their staple diet is pork and they hadn't been getting any 'cos it's never served in the foreign students' dining-room so's not to upset the bloody Muslim students. They reckoned they were starving. I say, Prof, that's an interesting point the Vice-Chancellor mentioned. He said the High Commission bloke told him people taste like pork, so it turns out when I thought the darkies were lusting after old Beefy the reason actually was …" Frewen rambled on but the Professor was no longer listening. Eventually he interrupted.

"You've told the police and the Vice-Chancellor about organising the dinner?"

Frewen started. "Good Lord, no – don't be silly, Prof. Had enough scrapes with the coppers in my time to know the ropes. Don't need any advice on that front! Golden rule – say nothing, if you get my drift. But that's not what I wanted to see you about. What's done's done. Like the Vice-Chancellor said yesterday: it's just nature taking its course – you know – bloody cannibals programmed to …"

"Mr Frewen, this is absolutely appalling; yet you seem to be taking an extraordinarily cavalier approach to it all."

Frewen adopted an injured look. "Can't see the point of crying over spilt milk. Nothing I can do about it now, Prof; and anyway, between you and me it's a bit of a relief. I bet you'd feel the same way too if it was you on servicing duty with old Beefy."

Just as Professor Trout began to reprimand Frewen again there was a knock and Angela Somerset popped her head round the door. "Oh, excuse me, Professor. Won't bother you. There's lots of policemen about so they must be raiding next door again. Just wanted to say I have a dentist's appointment at 2.30 so I may be a little late," and she was gone.

"I say!" Frewen exclaimed. "She's a cracker. Still, you want to be careful there though, Prof."

This was too much. "Mr Frewen! I've had as much as I can take. I do not indulge in hanky-panky with my students, nor anyone else for that matter."

"No, no, Prof. Wrong end of the stick. I mean her being

black. Like the Vice-Chancellor said, it's in their genes; you know, all this cannibal carrying-on. Never thought of academia as a dangerous job, but after old Beefy ..."

"Mr Frewen, I am happy to take my chances. I suspect the prospect of Miss Somerset roasting me is slight, to say the least."

Frewen shrugged. "Oh well, it's your call. All I can say is you'd have said the same about the New Guinea blokes two weeks ago. You can't be too careful with these coloured ones, if you get my drift. See, Prof, underneath they're not like me and you: not civilised at all."

Professor Trout thought rapidly. Under the circumstances perhaps decorum necessitated calling off his party. Then again, he considered, dreadful though it was, Frewen was right. What was done was done and life must go on. The function could not be postponed, as he was leaving for Scotland tomorrow. He would go ahead, and in the interim Frewen was the answer to filling the day until his guests arrived, if he could be persuaded to stay. It would certainly be a fitting end to his life at Ralston. "You mentioned you wanted to see me," he enquired. "I hope you don't just want to complain about overtime."

"No, no; not that – at least, that's not what I've come over for, although I still think we should do something about it if we get called out like that on Sundays," Frewen grumbled. "No Prof: need a bit of advice. See, things have worked out pretty damn good now old Beefy's off the scene, 'cept for a new problem. The Vice-Chancellor's made me the new Professor of Rubenesque Studies."

"Well, well, my heartiest congratulations! I'm sure you will handle it very well."

"I'm not worried about that. Got everything covered. The Vice-Chancellor accepted my advice and's made Sharleen Crudd a Rubenesque Studies lecturer, so she'll do all the work. The other lecturers were a bit shirty about my promotion so I need someone on deck I can rely on; plus we're really short-handed, with all the new enrolments. Good timing actually, old Beefy copping it last week. I was down for another protest this Wednesday, outside the Weight Watchers head office. Bloody Beefy said I had to break a window. Now Sharleen can do it." Frewen stopped suddenly. "Hang on a minute," he said excitedly. "Now I'm the Professor I call the shots. Maybe I should can the protests. Whatta you think, Prof?"

"I'm afraid I'm not really equipped to comment on that," Professor Trout said.

"Thing is, Prof, Beefy said it's part of the intellectual tradition. I don't want to cock things up in these early stages like my panelbeating professor's job. Was she right? You know: the 'intellectual tradition' stuff? I mean, you don't do it, do you?"

"No, Mr Frewen. Public protests are not part of mediaeval philosophy scholarship. They tend to be associated with other … if you like … less contemplative pursuits."

"And Rubenesque Studies: is that like you said – you know – less contemplative?"

"Indeed it is, Mr Frewen."

Frewen screwed his face up grotesquely to intimate deep thought. "Oh well, no matter," he said. "Sharleen Crudd can handle them. She can take over the essay-marking too, now I've created a new record. Haven't told you about that, Professor. I cracked the one-minute essay-marking barrier last week," he added proudly.

"Again my congratulations, Mr Frewen. You're an example to us all. But if you're abandoning essay-marking, what will you do instead – not to fill your time: I appreciate you have your television – but to keep yourself intellectually fine-tuned?"

"Writing a book, Prof. The Vice-Chancellor gave me Beefy's flat, which is owned by the University, so no more fat-lady duties on the home front for me. I hung all my beer mat collection on the wall this morning. Looks bloody good, too. You're welcome to come and have a look. Also, I found Beefy's Rubenesque Studies textbook manuscript last night, so I've taken it over and I'm banging in my conference speech as an introduction – you know, so as to put my own creative touch on it. Wouldn't be original otherwise. When I told the Vice-Chancellor this morning he got on the job pronto and told the University Press to publish it next month. He was very pleased; said it will help overcome any bad publicity for the Rubenesque Studies department over Beefy being eaten. New ball-game there, Prof, now they've got rid of that King fellow and replaced him with someone decent."

"Oh? Who's that?" Professor Trout asked, unaware that a successor to Walter King had been found.

"Chap called Mark Hourigan, headhunted from panel-beating lecturing. I reckon I'll cream it on the old royalties front, as it'll be a compulsory textbook. The Vice-Chancellor said he's keen on building me up in intellectual circles, so he told Hourigan it's to be called Frewen's Rubenesque Studies. He's putting on a big launch party for me when it's printed, and is going to be the guest speaker."

"So you need some advice about that, do you? What specifically is concerning you?"

"No, that's not what I want to see you about. That's all in hand. Matta fact, Prof, when I was looking through all Beefy's feminist books to get the hang of things I noticed they all had dedications to people for helping them write them. The American ones had two pages of names they thanked but they all had a special one on a separate page. Anyway, Prof, I thought I would dedicate mine to you – you know, for all the help you've given me."

Panic gripped Professor Trout such as he had never experienced in his six and a half decades of existence. He thought quickly.

"I believe that is the greatest honour ever paid me, Mr Frewen. I am enormously moved, to a degree I cannot tell you. However," and he paused to reinforce his next point, "it would, I deeply regret, be a very great mistake which might enormously harm your career."

This last ominous threat had the desired effect on Frewen. "Don't quite get your drift Prof," he muttered.

"It is absolutely essential in a textbook of such specialist scholarship that the dedication be to someone already respected in the particular activity."

"But who, Prof?" Frewen cried.

"I can think of no more fitting recipient than Professor Beefenstein. In respect of Rubenesque Studies she is your true mentor; and as, in fact, she has actually contributed to the book in respect of her notes, hand-in-hand with her unfortunate demise in the cause of Rubenesque Studies … well, overall, such a dedication would leave a first-rate impression."

There was a pause while Frewen weighed this suggestion. The Professor continued, concerned that Frewen might still be unconvinced. "My assistance has been of a broader nature, you see."

Frewen brightened. "Gotcha, Prof. You mean the beret and all that intellectual clobber stuff."

"Precisely, Mr Frewen. Now I suggest – indeed in the interests of your career I insist – that you dedicate the work to Professor Beefenstein; and if I may be so bold, when in the course of time you write your autobiography … well I would be enormously honoured by such a gesture."

"Righto then, Prof. I'll take your advice."

Greatly relieved, Professor Trout asked, "Now, is there any other matter I can assist you with?"

"Matta fact there is. That's what I'm here for. Just when I was thinking yesterday was the best day of my life a new problem's come up. See, Prof, last week Beefy said that because of me now being famous she was starting a new division to promote Rubenesque Studies and I was to head it up as Community bloody Outreach Director. Damned unfair, if you ask me, when I'd already got my hands full with the senior lectureship. So with Beefy off the scene I was off the hook and everything was happy again. But then the Vice-Chancellor said now I'm a full professor again, he's making me Dean of the Humanities faculty. Part of the build-up of my image, he said. He says the current Dean is about to retire. I kept mum of course: didn't let on I didn't know what he was on about, but here's the snag: what's a Dean? I mean what do I have to do? I fear the poo, Professor, just when everything's going so well with old Beefy out of the picture and no more bloody sumo and no community outreach stuff and me being a professor again."

Professor Trout gazed at him, thunderstruck. It was all somehow so fitting. After a pause he said, "Well, I suppose one consolation of this dreadful business is you won't have to continue with your excess eating empathy agenda."

Frewen shifted uncomfortably. "Could be a bit sticky dropping that, Prof. See, part of the deal for me fixing Sharleen Crudd up with the lectureship is she's giving me the cartons of pies her dad sends each week. Wouldn't want to hurt her feelings."

"You don't have to eat them, Mr Frewen," the Professor taunted.

"No, no, Prof: personal golden rule if you get my drift. Can't stand waste. Anyway," he added, relief crossing his face, "there's the hamburgers. Our department takes some of the output from the hamburgerologists to help them out. We knock off five each every day. Could look bad if I don't join in: you know, setting a poor example to the fat girls."

"I quite see your point," the Professor said. He decided to devote the next few hours to grooming Frewen – although, he reflected, "grooming" was not quite the right word when he studied his bloated form, ill-fitting attire and now long, straggling beard with its suspiciously Celtic ginger streaks.

"Do you know what humanities means?" he asked. Frewen did not, and for some time the Professor endeavoured to explain, but eventually concluded that helping Frewen become knowledgeable, if that was possible, would not in the event deal with the coping issue. He changed tack.

"Do you recall when you first sought my help? Apart from your clothing and the beret and spectacles and beard, did you adopt my advice about mumbling?"

"Funny you mention that," Frewen said, knitting his brow. "Been meaning to raise it with you. See, I gave it a lash and at first I felt a bit of a goose; but do you know, Prof: it worked. Everyone treated me quite decent – you know, not bothering me at all. Things became easy once I started all that head-down, talking-to-myself-out-loud stuff. I've often wondered if everything might have been different in journalism if I'd known about it, but we never had proper professional training like that. Whadda ya think, Prof?"

"A different field, Mr Frewen. I suspect mumbling might not apply to journalism. Doubtless that profession has its own behavioural procedures but I'm afraid that's outside my competence."

"Doesn't matter. Only asked out of interest. Academia's my right vocation. But it's a bloody worry now I've cracked it – you know, got a handle on the ins and outs of being a scholar – when the damned Vice-Chancellor then springs this Dean caper on me."

The Professor thought rapidly. "Your fears are unfounded," he said. "Stay clear of the history and the English and the philosophy … look, I'll jot down a list of the departments to avoid. You can't hide altogether so, to the extent you put in occasional appearances, ensure they're always in the vicinity of departments like sociology and Women's Studies and …"

"Do you think you could write a list of the good ones too please?" Frewen interrupted and Professor Trout did so.

"And you reckon that will do the trick?" Frewen appealed.

"Substantially, but not entirely," Professor Trout replied. "The critical element is to keep up the mumbling. Perhaps you could even step it up a decibel or two. Your beard is coming along very well, but you're not really safe until it reaches your stomach, so under no circumstances trim it. Also you could acquire a knapsack to wear all the time but it mustn't be new. Try the flea market again and find an old battered one."

"Scholarly, would that be, Prof?"

"Extremely scholarly, Mr Frewen. But unlike the beret, you should take the knapsack off when indoors."

"Gotcha, Prof; nothing else you'd recommend to deal with this Dean racket?" Frewen queried.

Professor Trout paused and thought for a moment.

"I suppose you could be seen carrying a tennis racquet every second day," he suggested.

Frewen looked perplexed. "Scholarly, would that be, Prof?" he asked again, only this time doubtfully.

"No, Mr Frewen: not scholarly, at least not in the knapsack sense. But it would deliver a certain frisson conducive to ameliorating any critical responses arising from your elevated status."

"Don't quite get your drift, Prof."

Professor Trout rephrased his explanation. "It would convey the impression of a man of many parts, a man of the world, a sophisticate, someone who ..." but he was interrupted by Frewen's brow-furrowed query.

"Snag I see is ... I never really learnt to play tennis."

There was a brief silence.

"Price of a busy life I imagine," the Professor suggested expressionlessly after half a minute had elapsed. "That doesn't really matter. Perhaps we should drop the tennis racquet proposition if you're not entirely comfortable with it."

Plainly relieved, Frewen nodded vigorously. "I could carry a dart, Prof," he suggested helpfully. "That's if you think a sporting touch would be a good thing."

"A dart? What do you mean?"

"You know, Prof – dartboards in pubs, all that carry-on. When Beefy made us take up sumo I told her she had the wrong end of the stick. Darts is what fat people play, I said, but she got all shirty about it so I shut up."

"I see. Perhaps she had a point. I may be wrong, but I suspect carrying a dart about would not be helpful. I'm afraid its purpose might not be readily discernible to casual observers."

"No other suggestions then, Prof?"

Professor Trout was now enjoying himself immensely. He fleetingly weighed transforming Frewen's image to that of an aesthete. There could be a summer outfit – a Panama hat, white linen trousers and shirt with the hint of a frill at the cuffs, and even a white silk scarf and an elongated cigarette holder. Frewen could carry a small silver cane or perhaps a puppy under one arm, which he could stroke with the other hand. In winter it would be black knee-high riding boots, polo-neck sweaters and a full-length fur coat with a Russian fur hat. He could carry a large volume of Virgil and peer into its pages from time to time. And in spring … but as the Professor studied Frewen's bloated dull-eyed form slumped before him, he quickly abandoned the notion. It was just too un-Frewen. For a start, he would be obliged to flounce rather than shuffle as he had been so painstakingly coached to do; and even were it possible to dandify him, which the Professor doubted, he would not in any event be here to provide the necessary tutelage. The Professor flirted with suggesting a kaftan but decided to leave Frewen as an eccentric don, although given his new status as Dean, further insurance was necessary.

"I think we might usefully add one more feature," he said. And for 45 minutes, under the Professor's guidance, Frewen shuffled up and down the study, head down, mumbling loudly and at approximately ten-second intervals, as instructed, jerking his right arm skyward while simultaneously emitting a falsetto shriek.

Professor Trout looked at his watch. His guests would soon be here for the party.

"I have no doubt you are now fully equipped to conduct a successful senior academic career in the new Ralston environment," he said, "but regrettably, you must now leave me. I have some matters to attend to, but before you go, I have a gift for you."

Frewen's eyes lit up. "A gift? I say, Professor, that's damned decent of you. No need to feel obligated, mind. Always happy to be of help when I come over, 'specially now as Dean I'll be your boss."

Professor Trout rose and rested his hand on the Plato bust.

"I'd like you to take this," he said. "The porters will shift it for you. You will find it a valuable tool in your new role as Humanities Dean. If you have any academic visitors from the philosophy or – you know, the bad list I gave you – then while you hear them out, stand with one hand resting on the head just as I'm doing and step up the mumbling. No need to bother doing this with any visitors from the good list."

"Sort of scholarly, would it be, Prof?"

"Very scholarly, Mr Frewen. You have my absolute assurance."

Frewen squinted at the bust. "Funny thing: when it was tucked away in the corner of your old room I always thought it was Churchill; but now I look at it properly … well Winston never had a beard, did he, and he was bald, so I suppose …"

"It's Plato," the Professor interrupted.

"What? Alfie Plato, the Leeds goalkeeper? No, Prof: Alfie's not bald and he doesn't have a beard. I was in the front row at his press conference after the under-age girl carry-on. Definitely not Alfie, Prof."

"Plato was a Greek philosopher, Mr Frewen. He lived 2,500 years ago."

Frewen looked relieved. "Oh! Righto then. I knew it

couldn't be Alfie. He's not Greek; not a philosopher either, I don't think. But thanks, Prof. I'll get on to the porters. Lazy buggers, they are. It'll give them something to do."

Just as Frewen reached the door a thought occurred to the Professor. "One moment!" he cried, and Frewen halted.

"Before you go, there's something I'd like to ask you. Tell me, Mr Frewen. What exactly is your forté?"

Frewen looked puzzled. "Don't quite get your drift, Prof."

"Your forté – your particular special talent – what is it?"

Frewen relaxed. "Ah, got you now! That's easy. It's scholarship. Just a pity I waited so long to find out. Being here at Ralston fits me like a glove."

"Of course," Professor Trout said apologetically. "Please forgive my curiosity when the answer is so obvious."

Professor Trout had not told Frewen it was his last day, and he watched from the window, for the first time with a sense of nostalgia at leaving Ralston, as Frewen, head down and mumbling loudly interspersed with shrieks as his right arm periodically jerked skyward, passed a group of policemen, now on to their third hamburgers. The officers shrank before Frewen's oncoming menace and seemed to meld together into a mutual protection group, caution and in some cases outright fear plain in their demeanour, until he had safely passed and they could resume their ghastly mastications.

Professor Trout opened the mail that was waiting on his desk. There was a letter from the Vice-Chancellor wishing him well in the future, and adding,

I have taken the liberty of providing you with a

wall-plaque of Ralston's new coat of arms as a leaving present. We are formally unveiling it next week. Going forward you will be able to display it on your wall as a reminder of your years at Ralston.

Professor Trout had always been rather fond of the symbolic trinity of Ralston's coat of arms. Introduced in 1826 after the university had added science to mediaeval philosophy and the classics, it was divided down the centre by a long-armed cross. The left side-panel showed a mediaeval scholar writing with a quill pen, and the right section three open books reflecting the university's then three academic disciplines. Underneath lay the inscription *Optima Durant*.

The Professor tore open the package and lifted out the new coat of arms plaque. It was divided horizontally across the middle, the upper half containing two panels, one displaying an open lap-top computer, the other, a vividly painted hamburger.

The bottom section showed a figure resembling Frewen, a mortar board on his head, pointing into the distance while behind him were a mass of eager-faced students. Underneath, etched on a curved ribbon, lay the message, Degrees for Everyone.

A small printed sheet of paper explained the new coat of arms. The hamburger represented Ralston's inclusivity in its approach to scholarship, no topic being deemed unworthy of higher study; the lap-top represented the new "bookless university" strategy, and the crowd scene, the universality of higher education.

Professor Trout dropped the plaque in the rubbish bin, just as the first of his guests arrived for his farewell party.

EPILOGUE

EIGHT YEARS HAD passed since Professor Trout arrived at St Andrews.

"Can I suggest you tackle this topic from a different angle," he said to his ten first-year foreign-scholarship students, who leant forward attentively, for there were no longer any British mediaeval philosophy students.

"You are all making the mistake in your essays of actually discussing the philosophic implications of the pantheistic outbreak among twelfth-century mediaeval philosophers. Don't you see how that is irrelevant?"

"Irrelevant to what?" the New Zealander Chris Gollins asked. "Frankly, Professor, it struck me as very pertinent to contemporary thinking in the Anglican church."

"Yes indeed, Mr Gollins. The comparisons are undoubtedly there, but that is not my point. To answer your question, your approach is irrelevant to our purpose as mediaeval philosophers.

What does that mean to all of you?"

"We study mediaeval philosophy to understand the philosophic propositions raised at the time," a young Indian woman proffered.

"No, Miss Singh, that is not what we do; at least not in terms of our underlying purpose. It could be argued that most mediaeval philosophy was philosophy in name only. Remember that it was almost entirely advanced within the confines of a prescribed religious doctrine and therefore could never be described as philosophy in its most fundamental Socratic sense, namely the pursuit of truth. Don't you see? The pursuit of truth is an illusory goal demanding an open mind and becomes automatically flawed if any inhibitions are placed on it. There must be no boundaries."

Professor Trout allowed this explanation to sink in, then, observing some puzzled looks he elaborated. "Let me present it more simply. Perhaps I'm confusing you by being excessively pedantic. For example, if every time a tightrope walker attempted his feat, he fell into the safety-net, some would say his persistent failure to complete the task disqualified him from describing himself as a tightrope walker. Others of a more charitable disposition might describe him as a mediocre tightrope walker, but would anyone be prepared to accord him the straightforward description of a tightrope walker? So too with mediaeval philosophers in terms of describing them as philosophers."

"If he never succeeds then I wouldn't call him a tightrope walker," Gollins said, and was immediately countered by another student claiming he would be a learner tightrope walker but still essentially a tightrope walker and that competence was irrelevant to his categorization. For five contentious minutes the debate raged as hypotheses justifying one or the other position were proffered.

Eventually Professor Trout resumed. "Regardless of your viewpoint on what is essentially a Cartesian dualistic dilemma, you will appreciate why some critics place the study of early mediaeval philosophy more under the broad category of history than philosophy. Where does its worth therefore lie? It lies, like all knowledge, as a valuable contribution towards understanding the human condition in all of its connotations."

"Just that?" a student asked.

"That is enough," Professor Trout replied, "but more particularly, the unphilosophic nature in a purist sense of most mediaeval philosophy does raise the chicken-and-egg proposition of the Dark Ages: that is, was one the cause of the other? Perhaps it doesn't matter to so speculate. What does matter is to observe the linkage, which is where scholarship enters the picture in drawing conclusions – such as noting how conservative negativity feeds off itself and breeds further negativity. Similarly, one might observe the linkage with the philosophers who were to come – Rousseau, Locke, Hobbes, Bentham, Mill or whoever – all of whom were able to advance their ideas without such restraints. Ipso facto the end of the Dark Ages, and instead, the Age of Enlightenment and the evolvement of widespread curiosity, leading to exploration, both physical and metaphysical; and with all of that, a vast improvement in the human condition. Or, closer to home, a former professor of our own Glasgow university, Adam Smith, and the advent of the Industrial Revolution and market economies and, in their wake, material progress. Equally we could revert to Aristotle and observe similar connections between his uninhibited philosophy and the broader thriving culture of the ancient Greeks."

Professor Trout waited while his pupils mulled this over. Eventually a Ghanaian student spoke. "So it's all about tolerance and freedom of thought, Professor."

"Oh yes indeed, Mr Tetteh. That is precisely what it's about."

"No restraints?"

"No, Mr Tetteh. Absolutely no restraints in the pursuit of truth. But remember the open-mind qualification. For that reason, by definition, no one can ever be certain they have found absolute truth. All one can hope to derive from searching for it is a sense of values personally appropriate to one's own life and conduct."

"So what you're saying, Professor," Miss Singh suggested, "is that in an open society we should always accord respect to every point of view and accept the validity of its expression, even if we don't necessarily subscribe to it."

Professor Trout looked out of his lead-mullioned study window. The late autumn sun was casting soft shafts of light across the facing ancient stone building, home of the university's music department. A remaining straggle of hardy, copper-coloured Virginia creeper leaves on its wall trembled gently in the slight breeze, but would soon join the rich gold-and-red carpet lying thick on the ground between the buildings. In two months winter would arrive; there would be snow on the ground and a fire in his study.

The Professor cast his thoughts back to his own personal Dark Age at Ralston, to the stark Humanities barracks, to Rubenesque Studies, panelbeating, astrology, paedophilia and the other Ralston new fields of study, and then to Frewen and the Vice-Chancellor. He felt blissfully content. He turned to the waiting students. "No," he said firmly. "Absolutely not. You are confusing tolerance with licence, Miss Singh. We most certainly should never automatically accord respect to every point of view, for such abandonment of value judgements opens the door to tolerance of viewpoints worthy only of contempt." Professor Trout paused and thought for a moment. "The western world endured the Dark Ages through excessive constraint. It is feasible that it could suffer another such period in a different form, through excessive licence. I said earlier – twice I think – that there must be no restraints or boundaries in the pursuit of truth. Perhaps I should have qualified that so there is no misunderstanding, for in fact there should always be restraints and boundaries. But," and the Professor paused for emphasis, "what is absolutely critical is that those boundaries are self-imposed and within the confines of reason and common sense, not from without. I would like you all to think about that."

Just then the sweet opening bars of a Mercadante concerto

wafted across from the music department. Professor Trout looked at his watch. "Time to call it a day," he said cheerfully. "Even though it's outside our mediaeval philosophy area of concern, tomorrow I shall take particular personal pleasure in discussing the important differences between tolerance and licence in the open society," and with a friendly wave he acknowledged Walter King beckoning at the window and left to join him for nine holes before dinner.

AFTERWORD

IN WRITING A SATIRICAL NOVEL ABOUT THE DEGRADATION OF universities from their former status as centres of scholarship with an emphasis on the traditional humanities, there are two points I wish to emphasise.

The first is that in promoting the humanities I do not assert that there is something intrinsically superior about philosophy, the classics, history or 17th-century English literature. There is not. Rather, such knowledge affords a solid foundation for understanding the human condition, and its acquisition is the best form of brain exercise.

The second point is that I may stand accused of snobbishness in wishing to see a university degree as an elitist symbol of scholarship, as it once was. I plead guilty and justify my position by arguing that standards count, that elitism in all endeavours is worthy of recognition and that anyway, snobbishness is simply a pejorative term for discernment.

Degrees for Everyone originally had a subtitle, 'A Glimpse into the Near Future'. I dropped it when academic friends told me that Frewenism is already thriving in our universities.